REYNOLDS

Also by Donley Watt

Can You Get There from Here?

The Journey of Hector Rabinal

Haley, Texas 1959

Reynolds

a novel by

DONLEY WATT

TCU Press

Fort Worth, Texas

Library of Congress Cataloging-in-Publcation Data

Watt, Donley.
   Reynolds: a novel / by Donley Watt.
     p. cm.
   ISBN 0-87565-256-5 (alk.paper)
      1. Middle aged men—Fiction. 2. Bankers—Fiction.
     3. Texas—Fiction. I. Title.

PS3573.A8585 R49 2002
813'.54—dc21   2001053140

For Lynn, again.

And to the memory of

Bill Shearer.

REYNOLDS

ONE

FROM THE after-hours darkness of the closed liquor store Reynolds stared out over the lake and waited for Joy. He was naked except for his jockey shorts and his socks. Everything—the shorts, the socks, even Reynolds—drooped just a little. A Corona sign on the back wall buzzed and gave off soft flashes that flickered across his hairy body. His skin, in daylight ruddy and creased, glowed white and smooth, almost blue under the neon lights. His chest rose and fell, rose and fell.

Reynolds took a deep breath, trying to slow things down, but instead set off another siege of hacking coughs. He almost dropped to the floor for another dozen push-ups, but thought "what the hell" and moved across the half-dark of the store, back to the front, for his cigarettes. He flipped the cassette in the boom box that was crammed under the counter. He lit up, inhaled, exhaled. Better. Reynolds reached under the counter again, found the fifth of Old Fitz 1849 and took a sip. Only the best is good enough for Reynolds, he thought, especially when you own the store.

The tape caught with a whir and Glenn Gould started softly, slowly, and for a few moments Reynolds felt himself stuck in a dark slough of melancholy. But when Bach's aria took off, Reynolds did, too, running softly through the store, sometimes frontwards, other times turning gracefully, moving backwards, his movements evolving into a dance. He high-stepped through the Texas wines up front, spinning past the mixers, racing down the long row of bourbons, "careful not to bump, careful not to bump," he whispered between gasps, catching glimpses of Scotch, tripping by the gin, righting himself, bowing to a display of tequila mix, then finally sliding fearlessly around a rack of Dallas Cowboy gimme caps, his socked feet solid and smooth on the wooden floor.

Breathless again, Reynolds stopped once more at the window that opened out over the dark lake. Clear Creek Lake stretched in its meandering way more than fifteen miles to the north from here. The lake followed the wandering bed of what had been Clear Creek, narrowing when it passed through the scattered hills, and widening in the flats. At the two narrowest points of the lake bridges connected the only paved roads that crossed the water.

Lake City Liquor Store perched on a hill next to the southernmost lake crossing, just a few miles up from the mammoth earthen dam, and it was seven or eight miles north from Reynolds' store to the next bridge. Built-in lake traffic, Reynolds had reasoned when he took over the liquor store.

The country around the lake had wilted this past summer, the last rain from a freak July storm more than three months earlier. Now, in late October, the lake receded gloomily from the sandy beach a hundred yards down the hill.

Reynolds owned the land all the way down to the lake, and once had figured he could charge a fee for boat launching there. It made financial sense—this inlet held the only protected boat ramp for several miles around—but Reynolds was too shrewd for that. You charge a fee, you have to hang around to collect the dollars, or hire someone to do it for you. Instead, Reynolds installed a four by six foot plyboard sign next to the concrete ramp:

> Boat Ramp Provided Free of Charge
> By Lake City Liquors
> Your Business Appreciated!
> Ray Reynolds, Jr.

Now in the darkness below him, Reynolds picked up the flash of a light. Someone was down there, roaming the beach. Probably trashing it out, he figured. Reynolds thought he could make out the silhouette of a man, and then a pickup truck. "Shit," he said aloud. Reynolds grabbed a broom that leaned against the wall and pulled it to his shoulder. He aimed the broom handle through the gleam of the window, down to where the figure moved in the gloom. "Dow! Dow! Dow!" he whispered, the straw end of the broom crunching into his shoulder with each shot. Then with a satisfied grunt he pulled the broom back down. The figure had disappeared.

Reynolds stepped back just a little and stared at his reflection in the tinted glass. In the muted light he still looked imposing—his hairy chest, the good bones of his long face not quite hidden by three days growth of dark beard. The hairs swirled around his belly button and climbed up his chest in a narrow stream, then spread and curled broadly below his neck, creating a pattern around the hardness of his nipples. For a moment Reynolds squinted his eyes, picking up the outline of some vague design made by the profusion of hairs. Then it came to him. He knew. "Yeah," he said with satisfaction. His growth of chest hairs had formed a Tree of Life, and Reynolds felt pleased, as if he had discovered the image of the Virgin of Guadalupe on a tortilla.

He backed up another step, feeling better about himself, now that he knew he carried on his body an ancient, almost holy image. Maybe things weren't so bad after all. He pulled his body erect, tried to force his belly flat. No way. But despite the unfortunate bulge in the middle, he was tall and lanky still. Six-three in his bare feet. Six-two-and-a-half, anyway, and he relaxed, felt himself droop once again. Maybe not so lanky. He sucked in his belly again, and held it as best he could. The darkness almost forgave his past few years of indulgences. Good strong shoulders, broad and tight. Knees a little bony, though, starting to have the pale, thin legs of an old man. "Shit," he said out loud. "Should put my jeans back on, before Joy gets here."

But Reynolds didn't move. Even with the a/c on high, even though the Shiner Beer calendar behind the cash register showed October, this was Texas. It might sleet day after tomorrow, but tonight was steamy and still. To hell with the jeans, he thought, to hell with the bony knees. Maybe I'll get down to Padre Island to catch some rays. Maybe Joy will take a couple of days off and go with me.

He took one last draw on his cigarette and stared out the window again, but now towards the narrow bridge that spanned this neck of the lake, and then on up the ranch road that disappeared over the far hill, now watching for Joy.

Bach made him sad. The Goldberg Variations especially. It was a strange sadness, a painful ache, one that gave him comfort. The strange comfort of melancholy.

The music spun in Reynolds head, a spiral that had begun

before memory, patterns of rhythm before there were words. His mama's hum, the "hush little baby, don't you cry, mama's gonna bake you an apple pie," a few early poems, again the rhythm more than the words, the rhythm planting the seed that would grow into a strange and comforting hybrid. "Ride a cock horse to Branbury cross, see a fine lady upon a fine horse," he murmured aloud. "Rings on her fingers and bells on her toes, and she shall make merry wherever she goes."

Reynolds thought of the women in his life. Sheila with her frosted, flipped-up-on-the-ends hair, her quick temper, her quicker tongue, and now, Joy, polluted with her chicken-fried world. Not exactly fine ladies on fine horses. "Shit, no wonder I'm fucked up." He laughed low, dropped his cigarette butt in a flower pot that held the shriveled, light-starved pad of a prickly pear.

Reynolds shrugged, not quite understanding. Willie Nelson had made Sheila sad, but that was years ago. Garth Brooks made Joy sad. Everyone was happy, it seemed, being sad.

Reynolds stared out over the lake, talked to his reflection in the window, the Goldberg Variations rushing over him. Who was Goldberg, anyway? And who was Reynolds? Well, for damn sure he wasn't who he had intended to be at forty-six. But he had survived. Not a banker now, but that had never been quite right, anyway. And the bank in town wasn't even a bank anymore, just the only barbecue joint in Cotton-wood with a vault and a drive-up window, the only cafe where a gum-smacking teenager took to-go orders from behind bullet-proof glass.

A car topped the distant hill on the far side of the bridge, still a couple of miles away, one headlight out. Reynolds checked the clock. 11:15, liquor-store time. That would be

Joy on her way back from Cottonwood. He had told her to get that headlight fixed. Speedeedle-um, speedeedle-unk, speedeedle-whatever. Reynolds couldn't remember, something from high school. Spot a one-eyed car and say speedeedle-whatever first and you get to kiss your girl. He could call Sheila out in Odessa. She would know. He shook his head. "Uh-uh, Reynolds," he said, the words ricocheting across the dark room. "That would be dipping deep into the barrel for old trouble." Speedeedle-uh-uh.

The Next-to-Nowhere Cafe, where Joy worked tables, closed at 10:00. The neon lights flashed and flickered in his mind the same way they had that first night he had waited for her there in the parking lot. Reynolds had slid down in the seat of his Lincoln and stared through the plate glass window of the cafe, like watching an oversized television screen that needed a good Windexing. Joy in her green uniform, Joy wiping down ketchup bottles, Joy filling salt and pepper shakers for the next day, all the while knowing that Reynolds was watching.

Joy was a pretty woman in a hard sort of way. Already she had developed a set to her jaw, and her pale green eyes were drained of trust. When she talked to Reynolds, she stayed busy at whatever, looking this way and that, so as not to get pinned down, trapped. Unless she wanted something. Then she would reach out and touch Reynolds on the arm, look him right in the eye, and go soft in an unnatural sort of way.

Joy's ponytail had swayed as she wiped down the tables, and Reynolds wondered what she was thinking, if her mind went beyond spilled sugar on the counter and the tips that hung heavy in the pocket of her apron.

Reynolds had no way to know, or maybe he knew all right. He had trained himself years ago to know things in his head, and keep them there, where they wouldn't seep down to his heart, to his gut.

Finally Joy disappeared off the screen, pitching a towel behind the counter, then untying her apron as she backed through the swinging kitchen doors. Joy tossed her head toward the cook, said something, and the big black man threw his head back with a laugh, then wiped his forehead with a smeared apron and grinned as she retrieved her purse from under the counter.

The next thing Reynolds knew Joy had banged her way out the greasy front door of the cafe and slid across the leather seat, her green uniform carelessly thigh-high, maneuvering over the seat belts until she was beside Reynolds, filling his car with the Next-to-Nowhere smells. Grease everywhere, overpowering the sweet staleness of Reynolds' cigarette smoke. Grease clung to Joy's ponytail, grease on her clothes. French-fried grease and chicken-fried grease and bacon and burger grease. Always there.

Even after she showered in Reynolds' trailer out back, behind the liquor store, the cafe's smells would linger while the trailer cooled down, the way it was cooling down now, while Reynolds hid out in the dark of the liquor store, while Reynolds danced and slid and spun around the aisles, while Reynolds smoked and sipped his bourbon and did a dozen push ups a set.

Joy would be here in a few moments, pull her one-eyed car in next to Reynolds' Lincoln Town Car, then fill the trailer with her Next-To-Nowhere smells.

From the window he could see the lake and watch the road, Joy's Dodge Dart racing down the hill now, rocking across the bridge in the still night. From here he could look back to his left and just see the end of the trailer where he lived, see his Lincoln Town Car parked there with its confetti vinyl top. Too many summers' sun, too many miles.

Reynolds felt himself sink. Had his life come down to this? Running a liquor store out on Clear Creek Lake, living in a trailer out back with a woman not much more than half his age, driving a car that was half her age.

It could have turned out better, had for a while. Down in Austin Reynolds had hooked up with Sheila, where they both were partying their way through the university. Sheila never was perfect, a little rowdy, not a take-home-to-mama kind of a girl. But she would barhop with Reynolds, most often leading the way. She knocked back her share of tequila and shot a mean game of eight ball. Sheila could be fun, could be crazy and wild, not a woman Reynolds had taken seriously. At first.

But before they graduated Sheila took Reynolds home for a round-up weekend at her family's ranch south of Odessa. This wasn't East Texas with a couple of hundred acres and thirty mama cows. This was 30,000 acres and imported Sussex cattle rubbing up against Permian basin oil derricks. Sort of opened Reynolds' eyes to possibilities.

Sheila's daddy gave Reynolds a ranch tour, bouncing all over sand hills and mesquite flats in his jeep, Reynolds worn out from hopping in and out of the jeep, opening and closing gates between the hundred pastures. Sheila's daddy eyed Reynolds carefully, right off asked him, "How in the hell you expect to make a living?"

"Banking," Reynolds had said. The old man spit to one side. "Goddamn bankers," he grunted.

Sunday afternoon before they left to go back to Austin, the old rancher took Reynolds aside. "Don't hang around those damned professors any longer than you have to," he said, his voice low, confidential. "A man can read too many books, you know."

Reynolds listened, fascinated by a thin, brown line of chewing tobacco stuck to the rancher's chin. He knew he had come to a crossroads in the cow path of life. One road led to a few more years of freedom, maybe a Dallas woman waiting for him somewhere on down the line, one a little softer, a better candidate than Sheila for marriage.

The other road led to previously undreamed of possibilities—a West Texas spread with built-in royalty checks. A man shouldn't have to face such choices. No man with Reynolds' weaknesses, anyway.

But after a few years Cottonwood bored Sheila. "Let's just go dancin' tonight, honey," Sheila would say, and Reynolds would go. He always could drink beer with the best of them, and after downing a few could even two-step a little. But never quite good enough for Sheila, who over the years started taking Larry and Garry, their twin boys, out to her daddy's place so "they could grow up West Texans." Sheila hated East Texas. "Too many people," she complained, "and most of them have funny looking heads."

Then in the eighties, when the grand jury started looking into loans, when the real estate appraisals by his used-to-be best buddy Dewayne Carter turned out to have more holes than a shotgunned SLOW sign on a country road, well, Sheila bailed out, went back to her daddy and his 30,000-acre blow-sand spread, took the money from the house her daddy had bought them, took the savings—what the lawyers didn't get—took the Range Rover, took the dog. Took Larry and Garry, too. That part not so funny.

Reynolds paid child support when he could, which was most months, maybe skipping January or February if the lake traffic slowed to nothing. It didn't bother Reynolds too much, knowing Shelia had her old man to fall back on. The twins would be okay. Better off there than here with Reynolds. He knew that, but still felt uneasy about the boys.

Reynolds ended up with a bunch of shaky land deals that hung in suspense until they crashed. He ended up with Lake City Liquors, a flimsy box of a store with a livable trailer out back.

But, now he thought, looking around, this hadn't been a bad deal. It was a good piece of property, would be if the lake ever took off. Not a bad deal at all, just didn't produce enough cash flow yet. Reynolds owned it though, by God.

He put his face close up to the window so that he could see the back half of the trailer and his car. Reynolds started talking once more, his voice angry, the reflection in the window now a stranger, now his enemy. He reached back somewhere for what used to be a full tank of pride, something he needed in order to keep it all going. Something that seemed to be running only on fumes now. "That Lincoln out back," he said, starting an inventory that turned into a litany, "it is mine. The trailer with that ripped-up apron and the family of racoons that live under-by-God-neath it, it is mine. The five inch hole in the ground that is the water well dug two hundred feet into the Wilcox pure drinking water sand, that is mine." He took a deep breath. "The sunken fifty-five gallon barrel out back is my septic tank, filled with my turds and my piss. This store," and with that he turned and waved one arm all around, "these bottles, enough goddamn liquor to float a sixteen-foot bass boat, enough beer to piss for a year. It is all mine." He took another deep breath.

"Damned pathetic," he said.

Out in Odessa Sheila had found herself what she called a

"rodeo-boy," a bronc rider/calf roper that had some years before been in the running for All-Around Cowboy. Sheila wouldn't tell Reynolds how many years ago. That didn't last for long. Sheila had called Reynolds one wine-soaked Saturday night a couple of years back, crying that her life wasn't worth a shit, no better than a stack of burnt toast.

"Rodeo-boy is gone," she said, "and I'm not crying over him. I'm crying over my life, wasted on two men already, and God knows what's next on down the road." Rodeo-boy, it turned out, was a little more his own man than Sheila could tolerate. "He wouldn't call if he was running two hours late," she told Reynolds, "unless he needed me to feed his cow dogs."

Reynolds had laughed and Sheila hung up. Reynolds hadn't always been punctual, either, but he always called, always had an excuse, a business conference, or he was making a deal of some kind or the other, and would phone from here or there, even if he had more than once zigzagged concerning his actual whereabouts. But for God's sake a man can only concentrate on one thing at a time, even if it is a third bourbon and water at the Midnight Express Bar tucked away in the back of the Holiday Star Motel.

Glenn Gould was frantic now, tearing through Bach in a way that only Bach himself might understand. Joy's one headlight flashed across the wall of the store as she turned in. Joy wanted her own place, Reynolds knew. At twenty-six she was too frisky to stay with Reynolds for long. This was a stopover, a place to regroup on the way up, to nursing school if she could make it, beauty school if she couldn't. The liquor store was a stopover for Reynolds, too, or had been four years ago, a way to grab onto something that he could own. "A liquor store," Sheila had said when he told her. "Well, at least booze is something you know." It was a place to put his last bit of cash, a way to never again be in a bank or a land deal. And something else, he knew, would come along, sooner or later.

But it was later now and what came along were the regulars and the fishermen, and an occasional fisherman's wife. He knew the drunks who couldn't hide it, the ones who no longer cared, the uneasy backsliding Baptists. Yeah, Sheila was right. It was something he knew.

The Reprise began, the notes clear, deliberate, slow. Reynolds moved with it—carefully, erect, drunk with emotion. The music ended without flourish and left him hanging for a dark moment.

Reynolds moved to the window. To his left the light from the trailer's bathroom splashed across the gravel of the driveway. Joy would be showering, scrubbing away at the Next-to-Nowhere grease, then toweling dry, dusting herself lightly with powder or smearing on cream or whatever this still strange young woman would do. Funny that he didn't know her well enough to guess.

At the edge of the lake he spotted the solitary figure again, this time moving slowly across the sand. A flashlight shone here and slowly over there. Then the light slid across the flat stillness of the water and held steady for a long time. Finally it went out. Reynolds wondered if there was a problem, if something had been lost, maybe something of value to that lone figure on the beach.

Then way out on the lake he saw the bounce of a red light as a boat made its way toward the dark shore, and suddenly the flashlight came on again, now the light dancing this way and that across the shallow inlet, signaling to whoever was out there, guiding the boat home.

Reynolds felt good about that, knowing that the unknown

person on the beach cared enough to fight off the sluggish October mosquitoes and help somebody make it safely back. Not trashing the beach out at all. He regretted he'd shot whoever it was with his broom.

The light from the trailer's bathroom blinked out. In a moment Joy slammed the tinny door behind her, headed his way. Reynolds ran his fingers through the top thinness of his dark hair, smoothing it along the sides where it still grew full and wavy.

Reynolds moved to the counter, found the Old Fitz and two glasses, poured three fingers in each one. He popped Glenn Gould out, slid Garth Brooks in. One, two, three. One, two, three. He began to waltz alone, spinning slowly toward the back door. Then he stopped, waiting for Joy.

❇   ❇   ❇

Joy had slammed the tinny door of the trailer behind her, kicked her sneaker into a corner of the back room. She jerked the green uniform over her head, popping a button that circled and then died on the vinyl floor. She talked to herself, a continuation and repetition of the talk she had with herself all the way back from the cafe. "I'm tired of goddamned waitressing, tired of goddamn Reynolds and his goddamn trailer."

Joy wadded her bra and panties into a ball and dropkicked them into the bathroom. She turned the water on high, as hot as she could stand it, and edged sideways into the tiny shower. She squeezed a handful of shampoo onto her hair. "And I'm tired of Reynolds being here every night, waiting for me, wanting to dance, wanting to screw. Well, screw him, I say."

Then Joy took off again, sputtering bubbles and water and foam as she ranted on. "Reynolds is a shit, a redneck, too, although he will try to convince you otherwise, playing that highbrow music, turned up loud like it was when I drove up a while ago. Get real Reynolds, I told him one night when he put that Bach mess on. This is Texas. You want some piano playing, I'll get you some real piano playing. I brought him a Marcia Ball cassette the next night. $12.99 it cost. What a waste. But the bastard listened all the way through with that sneaky grin on his face. He never even flinched, said it was great.

"But he can't fool me. I can see right through him and you can bet one of these days I'll tell the world what he's really like. He's a tomcat, a two-timer, a fraud, a schemer, a badass, a woman hater, a woman screwer, a pretend lover, a two-faced shyster. He dances like he waltzed in from the Dark Ages. Why I stay with him I'll never know."

Joy stopped to catch her breath. She frowned. "Yeah, shit, you do know," she said, still talking to herself. "Joy, you need to soak in a tub of Downy, hon. Soften you up. Things could be lots worse."

Joy dried off in the shower. She pushed open the door to let the steam out, let the cool in, open so she could listen to Garth Brooks while she dried off. She stepped out—hardly enough room to turn around in Reynolds' trailer—and wiped the little mirror with her towel. She brushed her wet hair straight, touched her lips with a little "Think Pink" lipstick. Just the basics.

Reynolds is sweet sometimes, she had to admit. The trailer was cool when she drove up, and he had left her kind of music on. He will have a drink waiting for her in the store. "He is funny, sometimes, and I guess he's smart. Or crazy."

She ran her towel across the mirror again. Her hair was still a tangle, roping off every which way. She pulled it back with one hand, into a frizzy ponytail. No way, hon, she said, and reached for the hair dryer.

Joy was living with a man twenty years older. But she knew what she wanted. "And for damned sure it's not Reynolds," she said, pointing the hair dryer at the mirror.

"Not for much longer, anyway." She closed her eyes and saw herself in a nurse's uniform, making double, maybe triple what she pulled down now even on good nights at the Next-to-Nowhere Cafe.

Joy dreamed of going home to her own house, one she owned or was making payments on, reclaiming Deanie, her daughter, from Joy's mama where she had to stay now. "Just until I get my nurse certificate," Joy said. "Not one minute longer."

But this was easy, and in January she planned to move up to Dallas to start nursing school. She would have to let Reynolds know sometime. Probably break his heart. Maybe she'd wait until after Christmas.

Joy knew Reynolds by now, what he wanted, what he liked. Knew him the same way she knew her customers at the Next-to-Nowhere Cafe, knew that UPS Carl wanted Tabasco with his eggs, knew that Real Estate Wilson wanted his hamburger burnt done, knew not to get cornered in the storeroom with Big Boss Bob. She was tired of knowing everything, being alert to what everyone else wanted, touching this one on the shoulder, laughing at that one's dirty jokes. Going through the motions to please, for extra tips, or like with Reynolds for a place to stay. To save 350 lousy bucks a month. "Might as well be an out and out whore."

In the fogged-over mirror Joy checked a little line of bumps on her forehead that seemed to have sprung up from nowhere. Reynolds' soap, she figured. Reynolds' cheap-ass soap.

Joy looked around, all of a sudden feeling trapped in the tiny bathroom, and moved into the trailer's only other room. She put one foot on the side of the bed and inspected her toenails. Nail polish just won't last when you walk a hundred miles a night, slinging 'taters, 'maters and meat in a cafe. What did she expect? And Reynolds would never notice, anyway. He wasn't interested in her toes. She knew that.

Then Joy picked up where she had left off. This was a nightly ritual, had been for the past couple of weeks, the shower melting away the cafe's grease and her talk bringing Reynolds down to size. She took a deep breath. "He's too old, too thick around the middle, has too much hair on his back, not enough on his head. His car's too long and hardly ever starts the first try. A Lincoln Town Car, older than Moses, he cruises around like he's still a big shot banker. And I hate that raggedy top."

She slipped on fresh panties, checked her breasts, held them up with both hands cupped, then slowly pulled her hands away. They hardly sagged at all. Joy slipped on her Cadillac Bar T-shirt and her jeans. Her feet hurt, too tired, too sore to even consider shoes, but sand burrs grew thick between the trailer and the liquor store. She slid her feet into an old pair of Reynolds' loafers and shuffled to the door.

The shoes didn't fit, of course. Reynolds was a big man. For Joy nothing seemed to fit right now, but she still could get where she needed to go. She stepped out the door, onto the landing and stopped. Garth Brooks crooned at her back. She figured that Reynolds and his weird music and whiskey waited for her straight ahead. She scrunched her toes to keep the loafers from slipping off and made her way down the trailer steps in the dark. She stopped for just a moment, stared up at the night sky. She tried to remember what it was like to be a little girl again, tried to remember that same sky from years ago. But she couldn't, and with a few awkward steps made her way across the weeds to the liquor store.

At the door Joy hesitated. From inside the liquor store she could just make out the lonely twang of Garth Brooks. She shook her head. "That damned Reynolds," she said. "He can be an old sweetie." And in spite of herself she smiled. Then with a deep breath Joy pushed open the door and stepped inside where she knew that Reynolds waited.

TWO

I T WAS almost dusk when Perry slowed his pickup and topped the last hill before the lake. He eased onto a graveled pull-off just this side of the bridge, cut the engine and waited. In the rearview mirror he checked the tarp-shrouded bed of the pickup and the trailer he pulled behind; no problems that he could see. When your cargo is sixteen fully automatic weapons and enough ammo to hold off a small army, you can't be too careful.

Perry stretched nonchalantly, then opened the pickup door, all the while eyeing his brother's Lake City Liquor Store lit up a half mile across the stretch of smooth water.

Perry waited for a couple of cars to pass, then watched while a pickup across the lake backed an empty boat trailer down the concrete ramp. The ramp stretched into the water a hundred yards down the hill from the liquor store. A ski barge bobbed just off shore; someone stood in the boat, balancing, holding a loop of rope.

They were loading up, Perry figured, would be gone soon, by dark, leaving the ramp for him and Snider. "Damn it," he muttered, thinking of Snider, hating the way he had to depend on someone to help who was so unreliable. But at least Snider was trustworthy, which somewhat compensated for his flakiness.

Perry's source for the weapons remained his own secret—not even Snider knew that. Perry could afford to buy only a few guns at a time, but it was incredibly easy. Last night he had placed a quick call, and this evening, just an hour ago, Perry met a pickup with a camper top behind a closed-down auto parts yard up the Dallas highway, just a half hour's drive from here. The gun dealers turned out to be a couple of ordinary looking fellows, one of them heavyset, the other a pint-sized, older man, by all appearances driving down to the lake for a day or two of fishing. Big D and Little D, Perry tagged them.

Where they got the guns, whether they were legal or not, wasn't his business, Perry reasoned. If he didn't buy the guns, they might sell them to some crazy. And now, with things shaky at school, Perry needed to put away what extra cash he could. So after a no-questions asked, ten-minute exchange, Perry headed back to the lake, where now he waited for Snider.

The rest would be easy—if Snider showed up—just a quick boat ride to the trail that led to his cabin, hidden deep in the woods that bordered the lake. And then a few trips back and forth from boat to cabin until the guns—with the others he had slowly accumulated—were secured.

Using the ramp below his brother's store entailed some risk, Perry knew, but the next boat ramp was up north at the Red Top Store and Marina and would require more than an hour's boat trip down the lake to get to his cabin. Reynolds would never see him, anyway. Perry knew his brother was too self-absorbed, mostly too drunk, or for certain, too busy sniffing around that girl shacked up with him in the trailer behind the store.

When Perry could hear no traffic coming from over the hill behind him, and saw that the long bridge before him was empty, he eased back to the boat, kicking the wheels of the trailer with the toe of his boot. Then he moved to the bed of the pickup and tucked the heavy, green tarp securely around its load.

The heaviness of the tarp, its faint odor of mildew and grass, reminded Perry of his Marine days. "The bastards," he muttered under his breath, then, catching himself, he glanced around to make sure he was alone, but the only movement was the flutter of a plastic sack the wind had trapped against a barbed wire fence out to one side.

Perry felt energized, antsy for Snider to show up so they could get on with this part of the mission. Until the guns were locked in the cabin—what he called his "safe house"— Perry would be on edge.

Perry liked that term, "the safe house." He had picked it up from some wimpy-assed women's deal he'd read about in the Dallas paper. But safe house touched something some- where deep. Not just safe for what he stored there, although that was important, the guns and ammo necessary, even for a show of force, if nothing else, when the conflict inevitably would come. But the safe house had turned out to be a place of retreat for Perry, now more often than before.

The safe house lay only a couple of miles from here, but Perry had chosen the almost the perfect spot for it. The land to the west of Clear Creek Lake, owned by a timber company in New Orleans, lay mostly in the flood plain. Its thousands of acres of scattered timber were accessible on the west side partially by a gravel road, and there only to the last high ground where a plank corral and barbed-wire catch pen had been built. Past that last point of high ground the land gave way on the east to an undulating sweep of land, filled after seasonal rains by broad pockets of dirt-churned water, seas of mud separated by an occasional rise in the land where cows and deer huddled together in small herds, waiting for the waters to recede.

From the east the only way to find the safe house was from the lake itself, and that required a boat and some reason to enter the narrow, shallow tributary creek that fed into the lake. Even if someone should venture past the low-hanging branches to the place where the creek ended in a pool, the trail to the safe house would not be apparent, hidden by the undergrowth of briars and a tangle of poison ivy vines and stands of wild dewberries.

The lake was huge, almost 40,000 acres, and it stretched more than seventeen miles from the dam to where it tapered out shallow in its upper reaches. On the lake there was boat ramp access in only three places, for this was Texas, with its legacy of private land rights, and only one of those three boat ramps lay in a public park, maintained by the county next to the dam.

Perry could have used that boat ramp, but it was too public, always busy with the comings and goings of fishermen and skiers, retirees who fished off the end of the pier, sometimes all night, eyeing everything that went on. At night, also, it was a place for kids to congregate, to drink beer and smoke dope and make out, always alert to the deputy sheriff and his stealthy cruises. And the lake shore next to the dam was open, cleared of trees for suburban-sized lots now dotted with log cabin-kit houses and added-onto trailers, and an occasional odd looking Swiss chalet A-frame.

There were two other boat ramps, the one far north of where Perry now waited, at the Red Top Store and Marina, but Perry's daddy had used that ramp for years, and Perry didn't want to risk running into Ray Senior up there.

That left only the lake access across the way, the ramp a hundred yards or so below his brother's liquor store, but a ramp, also, that was seldom used, almost never at night. The perfect place, as perfect as things go, except for Reynolds owning the land that gave Perry access. But he could deal with Reynolds if he had to. The least of his worries, as things were turning out.

Perry had to make this thing work, find a way to get support, convince more men to join him, find a way to wake everyone up before it was too late, before the multi-national corporations controlled it all, with big government smoothing the way.

But time might be running out, Perry knew, sooner than he had planned. In August the stupid high-school principal had called him in, handed him a letter from the superintendent imposing a probationary contract on Perry for this school year. "Teaching unauthorized curricula" was how they put it. But that wasn't it at all. Like most everyone else, the bastards couldn't stand to hear the unvarnished truth.

Over the years Perry had developed a political hypothesis that he called the Circle Theory. The political spectrum normally is textbook diagrammed as a straight line showing a left to right political alignment, the old leftist/rightist methodology with the neo-Marxists, say the Shining Path, on the far left and the Nazis on the far right, and that bunch of idiots in Washington and the national press celebs somewhere in the middle.

Perry's Circle Theory, the way he taught it in his senior

government class, is represented by a circle, with the leftists at the bottom, then moving clockwise filling in the United Nations, the One World bunch, then the Supreme Court, the Kennedy types, the mainstream Democrats, moving past the top of the circle and around, picking up the Republican party, the Christian Coalition, the John Birchers, the militia movement, and finally the Nazi skinheads.

What became clear was at the bottom of the circle the far left and the far right were separated by only a few degrees, more alike than unlike. They had no business being at opposite ends of a linear progression.

This was okay, but Perry pushed it farther, overlaid the circle with a new order that he had conceived, part libertarian, all anti-government. A system that filled in the center of the circle with small autonomous groups acting independently, but working for a common goal of national defense and independence. In this scenario the political parties we now know would be dissolved, along with the Congress and Supreme Court, both of which had misfired for over two centuries, trying to prove their worth, and had failed. A network of like-minded federations would run the economy, direct the government, protect their families and their homes from criminal intrusions—of all kinds.

Maybe Perry had made a mistake in teaching this, but change had to start somewhere. Perry could prepare all he could, organizing the network, arming the groups that he formed, but someone had to educate the followers, or it wouldn't work. A slap on the wrist is what he expected, the probationary contract at worst.

The school problem wasn't that bad, but Beth worried about it—wives always worried about the little things, Perry figured, unable to see the big picture.

Now Perry paced around the truck, lifted the hood to check the oil, then slammed it down, suddenly aware that a friendly deputy sheriff might stop to help if he thought Perry had car trouble.

He rolled the sleeves of his faded camouflage shirt up to his elbows. His forearms were tight, his freckled skin covered with a gloss of blond hair. Perry was blessed with strong features—a good chin, strong cheekbones, a broad forehead topped off with a no-nonsense buzz cut. A nice looking man; Beth had told him he was handsome. Maybe that's why he married her.

But his eyes were odd, one pale green, the other dark brown, which gave him a slightly off-balance look. Because of this Perry wore aviator sunglasses whenever he could, even now at dusk, with the sun out of sight below the tree line across the lake to the west.

Perry moved around the truck with a bounce, as if he could overcome being five-feet-ten by stretching with each step. His brother, Reynolds, had got the height of their daddy's lineage, while Perry had the lightness of skin and hair, the stockiness and strength from his mother's side of the family. Perry made the best of it, had played a mean fullback in high school, with his thick thighs and barrel chest and low center of gravity, ripping his way to an honorable mention all-state slot in his senior year.

He should have gone to college then, stayed with the scholarship he had. The Marines—all that humping with sixty-pound packs—had ruined his knees. Almost ruined his life. "The bastards," he said again. But he had come back, got his teaching degree in government, a minor in history. Cottonwood High School was proud to hire him. Ex-football star, ex-Marine. Just what they wanted. Even if no one there appreciated his unique grasp of the truth.

Perry slipped back into the truck, slid down a little in the seat, and adjusted the rearview mirror so that he could watch the road behind him. He had told Snider to be here at 9:00, when it would be good dark. Fifteen minutes more. He fiddled with the radio, punched his way through the stations. Stupid music. Stupid talk. He flipped it off.

From there Perry watched a customer with the last-minute thirsts drive up to his brother's liquor store, hurry up the wooden steps into the brightness of the store, and in a couple of minutes tote his brown bag out. Perry couldn't actually see into the store from that distance, but Reynolds' dinosaur of a Lincoln sat heavily on one side, out by the trailer that he called home. So Reynolds was there. Perry would have to watch it.

The lights in the store would keep Reynolds from seeing what went on in the dark outside, and the boat ramp wasn't lit, so he and Snider could slip out on the lake and back in without being noticed. Perry had brought a couple of rods and reels along for show in case anyone got nosy. Just a couple of fellows out after a stringer of bass. Night trolling, he thought with a smile.

A few minutes after 9:00 a car topped the hill behind him. He waited, still slumped down. The car, a Chevy Nova, honked—two faint beeps—as it cruised by. Snider. Perry straightened up and pulled out after him, following the Nova across the bridge. Perry's headlights picked up Snider driving and someone else close beside him. Shit, Perry thought. Some girlfriend, he figured. Snider should know better, but it was too late to back out now.

At the end of the bridge they turned and eased down a

gravel road. Perry drove past Reynolds' "Boat Ramp Provided by Lake City Liquors" sign and circled wide so he could back the boat down the ramp. He stopped and shut off the engine. The men got out, Snider striding quickly towards Perry, holding a can of beer lightly in one hand. Perry waited by the truck, his arms folded across his chest, shaking his head.

"I know, I know," Snider said, before Perry could start in on him. "She's okay. Brenda. She doesn't know and doesn't care. I told her we had to run a trotline. She's from Dallas, doesn't know diddly about fishing. Anyway she'll do what I tell her."

"Yeah, sure," Perry said. "Women always do what you tell them."

Snider laughed, flipped his cigarette at the darkness of the lake, made a sour look as he downed the last of his beer.

Perry frowned. Beer caused nothing but trouble. It had ruined better men than Snider. Had almost ruined Perry. And for an instant that night in a Philippine bar flashed through his mind. Funny how it was all clearer now than at the time. Perry could see, almost smell the smoke of the bar. He stood with a cue ball grasped tight in his hand, and Mouth twitched below him on the floor. It wasn't Perry's fault and it wasn't Mouth's fault. It was the booze.

Perry had tried to warn Reynolds about drinking one time, but his brother had laughed it off. Called Perry a do-gooder. If he could have told Reynolds about that night in the Philippines, how one drunken act can ruin your entire life, then Reynolds would have taken him seriously. But Perry didn't trust his brother that much, not with a truth that carried so much force. Maybe someday.

Now Perry and Snider moved quickly. Perry backed the

boat down the ramp to the edge of the water, then they both hit it hard, transferring the load from Perry's pickup to the boat without a word. Snider worked smoothly. He made his living as a framing carpenter, and now seemed to move effortlessly toting the long, wooden boxes from truck to boat. Snider wore jeans and a black t-shirt, an Oilers cap pulled down tight. A blond ponytail trailed down his neck.

When they finished, Snider moved around to the Nova, and handed a lighted cigarette through the open window to Brenda. Perry watched him shake his head, then say something. Brenda's voice whined a complaint that Perry couldn't quite get. Snider laughed.

"Snider," Perry spoke in a half-whisper. "Let's get going." Horny, whipped bastard, he thought. He made his way to the stern of the boat and fiddled with the choke.

Snider trotted down to the boat, leaned against it hard, and shoved it into the lake until it floated. He splashed a couple of quick last steps, and with a grunt hopped in the bow. Perry eased the motor down and started the little Evinrude with a quick pull.

The boat sat heavy in the dark water, and they chugged slowly out into the lake, then turned north, creeping along, only twenty yards or so off the dark shoreline. When Perry could no longer pick up the brightness of the liquor store on the hill above them he switched on the boat's running lights. With a spotlight Snider swept the water before them for stumps, and they made their way cautiously, still hugging the shore.

After half an hour Perry guided the boat up one of the narrow creeks that fed into the lake. They eased forward a couple of hundred feet, ducking under branches that drooped above them. Finally, when the creek narrowed to no more than a few feet wide, Perry slowed the engine, then killed it. With a paddle he pushed off one bank and then the other until the boat scraped the sandy bottom of a shallow pool.

Perry felt the heaviness of the moss and slime as he lifted the paddle. The rich aroma of rotted wood and leaf mold hung in the air. He shined the spotlight against the bank. "Watch for moccasins," he warned, as Snider stood and then stepped out on the soft bank.

"You worry too much," Snider grunted, and pulled the boat up as far as he could. Frogs croaked up and down the creek bank, and one, and another, and then another hit the water with a splash.

The men found the trail and followed it, pushing their way through the thick underbrush, their pants' legs hanging on briars and tangles of weeds that crowded the narrow path.

In ten minutes they came upon a small building, neither house nor storage shed, but a combination of both. The building, thrown together with odd rectangles of plyboard that had started to splinter and peel, was a box with a couple of windows on either side of the front door. A pair of heavy padlocks secured the door, and welded mesh covered the windows.

Perry unlocked the storage half of the building and eased inside, brushing away spider webs, checking the floor with his light for snakes and scorpions. He played the light around the room. Shelves of canned goods and jugs of water took up one side, and stacked crates of ammunition of different calibers rose high in a far corner. A couple dozen guns leaned against the back wall. "Pretty impressive," Snider said. He hadn't been out here for several weeks.

"When the shit hits the fan," Perry said, "and it will, we'll be ready."

The two men worked in tandem, back and forth along the narrow trail, Snider pulling the crates of guns and ammunition from the boat, staggering the few steps through the mud, and depositing them heavily on the dry, high ground. Perry hoisted the crates, one at a time, on his shoulder and made the trek to the safe house twice before Snider had finished unloading the boat and could help.

Together, they stacked the crates on two-by-fours to keep them off the wooden floor. The night was still and mosquitoes worried the stale air of the safe house. When they had finished Perry shined the light around, checking their inventory.

"What happened to the AK47s?" Snider asked. He tapped a cigarette from a package, stuck it between his lips, but didn't light it. "There was a dozen of them last time I was here. Over there. In that corner." He moved to the far wall.

Perry flashed the light next to Snider just for a moment, then waved it towards another crate. "I traded up," Perry said quickly, trying to keep his voice even.

He had traded up, in one way of thinking, moved the dozen automatic rifles for cash, to some fellows from Waco he had located through an ad in the back of Gun and Ammo magazine.

At the time Perry figured that one deal would set him up, let him pay some overhead for the operation, provide a little operating capital. But Beth had been on his back about some credit card bills that seemed always to stay the same, and Perry used the last of the gun money to clear those up. Things had gotten a little out of hand, Perry knew. But he had needed the cash, and how many guns could they use, anyway? This was a small potatoes operation. The unit he headed had less than a dozen men in the entire county. Only five or six he trusted, felt he could count on. Snider was one of them, and even he tended to be careless. A couple of the others were loose cannons, hotheads looking for a fight, and another three hadn't proved their loyalty to the cause.

So twice in the past few months Perry had delivered a load of guns, both times coming out alone in his boat to the safe house, then right at midnight meeting his Waco connection back at the boat ramp. Each time he transferred his tarp-covered freight into their van and pocketed an envelope of bills. It was a no-questions-asked kind of deal.

These fellows—there were three of them—were pros. They would show up at the boat ramp in that metallic blue van with tinted windows all around, a strand of fringe dangling across the top edge of the windshield. A miniature Virgen de Guadalupe rode prominently on the van's dash. A skinny fellow drove and helped Perry transfer the guns. He had a bony face with the few scraggly hairs of a goatee. He kept a Miami Dolphins cap pulled down tight on his head, and blue-black hair curled up all around the cap. The guy has some nerve, Perry thought, wearing a Miami Dolphins cap this close to Dallas. But he seemed to know what he was doing.

The skinny fellow packed the guns, two at a time, in long white florist cartons marked "Fresh Flowers" in bold red letters.

When they were done, the driver passed Perry an envelope of cash through the window of the van. All Perry could see was the top of a head, a thick arm, a fat, brown hand. A drift of cigar smoke escaped through the window, and the shadow of another figure sat quiet and still in the back seat.

Skinny and Fat Hand and Shadow, Perry tagged them to himself. Names freely given would be names invented, so no one bothered with the form of lies. What's a nice guy like you doing with sleazebags like this? Perry had asked himself with a little laugh. But the laugh was uneasy, and the trio of gunrunners gave him the creeps.

On those nights Perry could have used Snider watching and waiting at the other end of the bridge, ready to flash his lights if a deputy sheriff cruised by, keeping his eye on the liquor store for any late-night activity. But Perry didn't want any partners when he moved the guns. And, besides, Snider would be too far away and no help at all if the fellows in the van gave him trouble. But trouble happened to the dumbasses, the careless. If you keep things clean, do what you say, then they deliver the money, and you deliver the goods. Trouble was only something that happens in the movies. Those jerks in Hollywood wouldn't know how to handle this, with no drugs, no shootouts, no bad guys. Only bad laws. Too complex for those La–La land bastards.

After a minute the big fellow on the passenger side of the van would grunt and they would pull slowly away. The van's tires would spin, city tires that slipped, losing traction, spitting a little gravel that peppered Perry's legs. Then they would swing right at the highway and move slowly past the liquor store and out of sight.

Mexican. Perry had thought at first the three men in the van were Mexican, but now he wasn't so sure. Colombian, maybe. He had worked with Mexicans, felt easy with their mannerisms, their cultural idiosyncrasies. But the skinny fellow had something peculiar about him, the way he lifted the cartons, the way he stood and waited. Maybe his voice, the so-so English. And the music that drifted low from the van, so low he could hear it only when at last the window slipped down just a couple of inches and the rush of smoke, cigar smoke, filled the air around the fat, brown hand. The drift of music not conjunto or ranchera or salsa. Something more from the islands. And then it came to Perry. Cuban. Maybe they were Cuban. Shit. He didn't want to deal with Cubans, help those Castro commies. Or maybe they were anti-Castro, and had connections in Miami. But maybe not. He would see them again.

This was a slow process, but Perry would be patient. You buy a dozen guns, a thousand rounds of ammunition, then you move ten of them, with seven hundred rounds. You're two guns ahead, maybe a little cash if you're lucky. All it costs is a couple of nights on the lake.

Perry saw himself as a middleman, an expediter. It had happened so seamlessly that the word gunrunner would have brought from him a quick laugh, a look of astonishment. A gunrunner? Not Perry.

It was almost 11:00 when Perry and Snider made it back to the boat ramp. As they neared the landing a flashlight beamed their way from the shore. "Shit," Perry whispered.

"Hell, it's only Brenda," Snider said. "Besides, we're clean. Damned turtles stripped our trot line." He laughed.

"Yeah, but I still want to keep it quiet." Perry stared up the hill at the darkness of the liquor store. Reynolds had closed the place at 9:00—that was the state law—and, Perry figured, would be out back of the store in his trailer, slumped down in front of the TV, or maybe screwing that girlfriend of his. If she hadn't already left him. But the trailer was dark. No light at all. What he didn't want was Reynolds wandering down the hill to see what was going on.

Perry pulled back on the throttle, the boat rocked forward

and went into a quiet glide. "Kill the damned light," he yelled hoarsely at Brenda.

But the light stayed on, playing across the water in front of the boat, and for a minute Perry was afraid it might not be Brenda, but Reynolds.

But then Snider spoke up. "Kill the goddamn light, Brenda," and the light went off.

"I was only trying to help," she said. "What took you so long? It's scary out here, and the mosquitoes are awful. I'm never coming out here again."

"Promises, promises," Perry muttered, and Snider laughed.

"Did you keep that beer cold?" Snider asked, as they bumped against the shore.

"That's all you care about," Brenda said. She wheeled around and hurried back towards the Nova.

"Not quite," Snider said. Then he turned to Perry. "But beer's a close second." He laughed, but Perry didn't.

"Don't bring your women out here, Snider. It causes nothing but problems. And drink your beer at home. Last thing you need is a DWI, get the sheriff watching this place."

"Hell, Cap'n Perry," Snider said, his voice tight. "Ease up. A beer might not be bad, mellow you out a little."

"No loose talk, and no women," Perry said. "Not out here." Then he lightened up. He needed Snider. "Come on, old buddy, what we're doing is bigger than a six pack and a strange piece of ass."

"I know, I know," Snider said. He stepped out and pulled the boat higher on the ramp, jerking it hard.

Perry made his way to the front of the boat and hopped out. He eyed the Nova where Brenda waited, slouched down in the seat, listening to the whang of some sad song that drifted out the open car window and into the night.

For a moment he wished that he was Snider, and he tried

to imagine what it would feel like to slide behind the wheel of the low-slung Nova to the sweetness of cigarette smoke and the soft glow from the radio and the whangy crooning beaming out from some Top Forty country station. The car filled with longing and too much perfume. Sliding in, stroking Brenda's thigh while she popped the top on a cold Lone Star. That first sip of cold foam, then a swallow and another of the bitter golden beer. Then the lightness, everything falling away, and you rev the engine in a cool sort of way and rumble up the gravel incline to the highway where you turn out, not too fast at first, drawing a sensuous murmur from the twin glass-packs, the wheels slipping just a little on the gravel until they catch and propel you north with the wind whipping through the open windows, and Brenda slides over close and lays her hand playfully high on your thigh, her fingernails scratching lightly.

"You okay?" Snider asked, jarring Perry back.

"Strategy," Perry said quickly. "Always planning my strategy."

Snider shrugged and Perry slipped him an envelope. "Just remember where this comes from," Perry said softly.

"How could I forget? But, yeah. Thanks. And I'll take care of Brenda. Don't sweat it."

"I sweat everything," Perry said quietly.

They cranked the boat onto the trailer and took off, Perry leading the way, his eye on the liquor store above. When he got up the hill and onto the paved road, he turned the pickup east towards Cottonwood.

At the top of the hill he met a car with only one headlight and flashed his own lights to bright and back to dim, a signal the other driver ignored. "Damn broad," he said, when the one-eyed car whizzed past him and he caught a glimpse of the driver, her hair twisting in the wind.

Perry's mind moved to Brenda again, and Snider. Maybe she hadn't slid over next to him at all, maybe she was pissed and stayed hugged up against the door on her side and pouted all the way back to town where Snider unceremoniously dropped her off at her place and drove on home alone with what was left of his now-warm six-pack. Yeah.

Perry didn't have it so bad. Actually Beth was better looking than Brenda ever would be. A better mother, a better woman in every way, Perry suspected. "Perry Reynolds," he said out loud. "You're one lucky son of a gun." But he could hear the half-heartedness in his words.

It was half past 11:00 by the time Perry cruised through the blinking yellow lights in town, and then covered the five miles of farm to market road that led out north of Cottonwood to his house. He backed the truck up, maneuvering the boat under the carport, next to Beth's van, and killed the engine. The house was dark.

Perry closed the truck door softly, holding the door handle out, and pushing the door closed until it just caught. By now the half moon had risen, and his low ranch house took on an eerie contrast of shadow and luminous glow.

On the front porch he kicked his mud-caked boots off to one side and let himself in. He waited a minute just inside the door, listening. Nothing. Then his eyes adjusted to the dark of the house, and he picked up a thin line of light under their bedroom door.

Dammit, he thought. If Beth had fallen asleep reading, he might make be able to flip the light off and ease safely into bed. But if she was awake, waiting for him all in a stew, then slipping into the room would only make things worse. He could undress down to his shorts and crash on the sofa, or maybe. . . .

But just then the bedroom door swung open wide and Beth faced him, not sleepy at all, but with a hurt look, a familiar hurt look, on her face.

"Do you know what time it is?" she asked. "I don't care where you've been, but folks will be waiting outside my office at eight o'clock in the morning, and they won't care if I worried half the night away wondering where you were." Beth stood with her arms crossed, wearing Perry's old pajama top with the sleeves turned up.

Perry wanted to say something to soften her, make her laugh. They would make up over a glass of milk and a left-over piece of pie and maybe Beth would slip back into bed with the pajama top unbuttoned all the way down, her signal to Perry that she wanted him. But Perry could tell this wasn't going to happen. Not tonight.

Beth had wide set eyes, dark brown, and they always, even at her most relaxed moments, held a look of slight astonishment, of surprise. But tonight the wide-eyed look was more of anger than surprise.

"Beggar's lice," she said, pointing at Perry's pants' legs. "You take your boat and supposedly go out to the lake fishing, and end up with beggar's lice all over you."

She moved closer to Perry, reached out and took his hands. He pulled back. "You caught some fish, I guess, so your hands must smell like fish, or at least like lake water, or bait. Don't they?" She tried to pull Perry's hands to her face, but he jerked away, backed off, wiping his hands on his jeans as if that would cleanse him in some way. Then he strode around her towards the kitchen, bouncing on his socked feet as he went.

Perry stopped at the refrigerator, hid stooped behind the open door for a moment, sucking in the cold air. He

straightened up, took a long drink from a jug of orange juice.
More than anything else Perry wanted to be left alone, to
close everything down, go to bed and sleep a dreamless sleep.
But Beth wasn't going away. Not yet. He would have to reason with her. She hated his rational arguments, Perry knew,
but they would finally wear her down. If he could just keep
her off balance for a little while she would give up and in the
morning he could hurry off to school early. Things would be
better after that.

"First of all," Perry said, as he straightened up, "I don't have
to explain anything." He started to pace around the kitchen,
but felt trapped, hemmed in. He drew on his best classroom
voice. "I am a man," he said, his voice humming, "and I have
my own ways. As long as I work at my job, honor our marriage, and am a responsible father, then my time, my other
work—which you could never understand—is my own
business."

"This isn't the Dark Ages, Perry. You can't keep me in the
back of a cave, you know." Beth's astonished eyes glittered.
"And there's more to a marriage than going through the
motions, following some rule book you've made up in your
head."

Perry put a finger to his lips, gestured towards the back of
the house, where down the hall their daughter, Jennifer, slept.
"Okay," he said, "I didn't go fishing. I admit it. I don't give a
hoot for fishing." He took a deep breath. "What I'm doing is
not for me, but for you, for Jennie." He groaned, a little the-
atrically he knew. "I don't want Jennie to grow up in the
world I grew up in, where only the rich are empowered,
where arbitrary and unfair rules keep ordinary folks like me
beaten down, where the money we earn is taken away and
given to foreign dictators and world organizations to support
the lazy and the slothful, the un-Christian and the corrupt."

Beth sighed. She ran her fingers through the tight curls of her dark hair. She shook her head from side to side and Perry was afraid she would scream. She pointed her finger at Perry, jabbing through the bright air. "I'm sick of your know-it-all speeches." She sagged a little, her shoulders falling, her eyes tearing up. Perry felt like an asshole, knew he should comfort her. But he couldn't say a word.

"Can't we just live?" Beth pleaded. "The way other people live? With good jobs and a nice enough house and a healthy, wonderful daughter. Isn't that enough?"

Perry sank inside. How he would like that. To be an ordinary man with ordinary thoughts and an ordinary acceptance of his life. "Injustice and immorality and dishonesty and evil will not just go away," he said. "They, too, are ordinary, and they, too, I will not accept."

"You died in the Marines," Beth said. "When you hit that poor Marine in the head, when you killed Mouth, the Perry Reynolds that I knew and loved died, too. Only I didn't realize it until now." She turned towards their bedroom, then stopped. "I feel pity for you Perry. You're going to lose everything you have." She waved her arm around, taking in the whole house, the whole world, it seemed. "Everything." She slipped into the bedroom and closed the door. But the thin line of light glowed from under the door for a long time, long after Perry had picked the beggars lice from his jeans, and had fallen asleep on the soft pastel swirls of the sofa.

THREE

WHEN the phone rang at 8:30 Reynolds was awake, but still in bed with Joy. The night before hadn't worked out for Reynolds— not that it was all Joy's fault, ground down from the late shift at the Next To Nowhere Cafe, and not his fault either, sipping on that Old Fitz until half past mellow, waiting for Joy to show back up.

Things might be better this morning, he figured, with Joy rested up. Reynolds had waked up horny. Hangovers did that to him, it seemed. He turned towards Joy, careful not to move too fast. He slid his hand under the tangle and twist of sheets, ran it along the warm silkiness of Joy's inner thigh. Smooth as a catfish belly, he thought, hoping Joy might wake to his touch. Reynolds slipped the sheet down a little, nuzzled the back of Joy's neck, her hair in his face. Reynolds inhaled a mix of shampoo and smoke and his own stale bourbon breath. Joy moved, grunted some lower vertebrate animal sound, and wriggled deeper down in the bed. Not encouraging. That's when the phone rang.

Shit, Reynolds thought. He rolled over, annoyed, and reached for the phone. No one called this early. No one he wanted to hear from. "Junior?" It was a woman. Not a young woman, however, and Reynolds sagged. Only kinfolks and old high school buddies called him Junior anymore. "This is Reynolds," he said. "Thank goodness," the voice said. "Junior, this is Dottie Hairston. You'd better come home. I think your mama's gone crazy." Dottie Hairston lived next door to Edwina and Ray Senior, Reynolds' mom and dad. Dottie had been a neighbor since before Reynolds could remember, although for years she and Edwina had been more over-the-backyard-fence squabblers than friends.

"Now, Dottie," Reynolds said, trying to keep his voice even. "I am home." He looked around the trailer; from the bed he could see the coffee pot upside down on the drain board by the sink, and breakfast on the table—two cellophane-wrapped Honey Buns Joy had sneaked out of the cafe last night. A couple of bath towels hung across the back of a dinette chair. Home, damned sweet home, he thought. He leaned back on the bed, resting his head on the hump Joy's ass made under the sheet. Joy didn't stir.

"Don't give me any smart talk, young man," Dottie said, and Reynolds felt a rush of guilt from being scolded. "I'm only trying to help. Edwina's gone crazy and somebody has to talk to her. Willy Elmer, that nigra boy, is in her backyard, chain sawing down all those pecan trees." Dottie let out a dramatic sigh. "Oh, those magnificent trees. Destroying the bountiful blessings of nature." Dottie Hairston had taught second grade for forty some-odd years, had even taught Reynolds umpteen years before, and had a weakness for words like "magnificent" and "bountiful." Reynolds' daddy, Ray Senior, had tagged them "Dallas words," Dallas being an altogether different nation-state, wholly separated from Cottonwood, although Big D was only a straight seventy mile shot to the west.

"Maybe Mama wants to cut those trees down," Reynolds said, feeling contrary, angry that Dottie Hairston could reduce him to a second grader again when they talked. "Maybe if you asked her, she'd tell you why. Maybe she's not crazy at all." But Reynolds knew that Edwina had her tendencies. He cleared his throat. "And I am tied up right now, you know, business to take care of and all of that." Reynolds held his now limp manhood while he talked, hoping it might stir back to attention. But talking to Dottie seemed to erase even the possibility of fornicating.

"I tried to get your daddy, but the boy at the car lot said he'd taken someone for a test drive. To the Donut Palace, more likely than not." Disdain in her voice. Then she continued, softer, gentler. "And Perry's always so busy." She always liked Perry best. Everyone always liked Perry best. Reynolds sighed. Dottie sighed. "You're the only one who can do something. Edwina will listen to you. I hope."

Well, call Perry, Reynolds thought. Get my little brother over there. It's Saturday. There's nothing sacred about being a goddamn schoolteacher, anyway. It's just a goddamn job. No more honorable than running any kind of business. Even a liquor store. The truth be told, running a liquor store might do more good.

"Thirty minutes," Reynolds said with a sigh. "Maybe forty-five."

"They'll all be ravaged by then," Dottie moaned. "The

destruction of those marvelous trees. Those gifts from God. The shame of it all."

"Dottie," Reynolds snarled, "there's been a lot worse shame in our family." He touched the off switch on the phone, held it down a few seconds, and stuck the receiver under his pillow. Then he reached for Joy.

※   ※   ※

By the time Reynolds made it into town, his daddy's Ford pickup was backed into the driveway and Ray Senior was shoving boxes around in the slick bed of the truck. Ray Senior stopped when he saw his son coming toward him. He nodded and eased down on the open tailgate.

"Junior," Ray Senior said, fiddling with a cigarette he'd just rolled. "I'm glad you showed up. Madam Queen's sittin' high on her throne, for sure." Ray Senior gave a little laugh that turned into a hacking cough. He spit to one side, and wiped his chin with the sleeve of his khaki shirt. He reached into his top pocket and pulled out a book of matches. "But her crown's a little cockeyed today." He looked at Reynolds. Took him in. Up and down. "Son, you look like hell."

Reynolds ran his hand through his hair and moved closer to the pickup. Besides the boxes, the back of the truck held a couple of rods and reels, Ray Senior's beat-up tackle box and a floating minnow bucket. One of the boxes held an iron skillet and enamel coffee pot singed black from campfire soot. "You going fishin'?" Reynolds asked. "Out to your cabin?" Reynolds knew about his daddy's cabin, although he'd never been there. Across the upper reaches of Clear Creek Lake, the cabin was stuck way the hell back in the Trinity River bottom. A place Reynolds' daddy had retreated to over the years when his skirmishes with Edwina broke out into wars.

At that moment a chainsaw sputtered reluctantly from the backyard, then roared to life. Ray Senior raised his voice, almost shouted at Reynolds. "Fishing? Yeah. Going to do a lot of fishing."

"God awful bunch of stuff for a fishing trip." Reynolds eyed the boxes loaded in the back of the truck, stuffed with tools and clothes. An army surplus tent was wrapped around something bulky. Reynolds reached over, touched the tent, looked at Ray Senior.

"My machine," Ray Senior said, his voice a hoarse whisper.

"Oh, yeah," Reynolds said. He knew about his daddy's invention that had never quite worked. "Your perpetual motion machine."

Ray Senior put one finger to his lips, glanced around to see if anyone might have overheard Reynolds. He waited while a yellow dog padded by, sniffed at the base of a hackberry tree, lifted a hind leg and left its mark. Ray Senior didn't trust anyone when it came to his invention, not even a yellow dog.

Ray Senior had worked on this machine for years. He secreted it in a storage shed back of the garage. Kept the shed locked. Once the machine had worked for three weeks, and Reynolds had stopped by a couple of times, studied its jerky pendulum motion, tuned in somehow to the electromagnetic rhythms of the earth. An "internal energy system of unidirectional force," Ray Senior had explained. "Based on the technical, gyroscopic mode of inertial propulsion." Reynolds had been impressed. For a Ford pickup truck salesman, his daddy sure knew his stuff.

But still there was a hitch somewhere, and the machine

slowed imperceptibly over time. "A problem of friction and gravity," Ray Senior had observed, "the loss of momentum is so damned gradual that it can't be measured, in the same way that a tree can't be seen to grow."

"How long you gonna be gone?" Reynolds asked now.

Ray Senior shrugged. He held the box of matches in his hand, turning it slowly over and over. The unlit cigarette dangled from his lips as he talked. "Gotta finish my machine. I'll stay there 'til she's done. Then I'll see. Shouldn't take too long. She's almost there. I get her perfected there's no telling what I'll do. Don't count on me ever showing up here again. But for now I need some place out of the way." He glanced around once more, leaned close to Reynolds. "Got to keep this thing quiet. Exxon, Mobil—they get wind of what I'm doing and it's all over. This machine will ruin 'em in a Dallas minute. No telling what they'll pay to buy me out."

"Let me talk to Mama first," Reynolds said. "Before you take off."

"Go ahead," Ray Senior said. "Won't do any good." He picked a brown flake of tobacco from the end of his tongue. "You will ride out with me, won't you? I'm headed out your way. To the lake. To my boat."

Reynolds knew his daddy had a little bass boat tied up at the Red Top Marina on the lake. Not that far out of the way for Reynolds, but he hated spending thirty minutes alone with his daddy. "You can leave your pickup there, can't you?" Reynolds asked. "Old Man Tyner will keep his eye on it, won't he?"

"Not for as long as I'll be gone," Ray Senior said. "Son, you can run my truck back into town. Leave it at the Ford place. Buddy Miller out there will move it for me if I'm not back in a couple of months. I'm cuttin' rope."

"Lots of rope to cut," Reynolds said.

"End of the goddamn rope," Ray Senior said. He jerked his thumb toward the backyard. "Yeah, Madam Queen's too much for me. I should have taken off years ago."

Ray Senior glanced over at the house, gave it a wave. "Adios. Sayonara to all that crap. Fourth and long and I'm punting."

Reynolds checked Ray Senior's stuff. It only half-filled the bed of the truck. "Pretty good load for a fishing trip, but a tad slim for the duration."

"More than enough for an old man."

Reynolds looked closely at his daddy and for the first time maybe ever paid attention to what he saw. Ray Senior was nearly seventy and showed it, the droop of skin under his eyes, the blotches on his face, his hair combed straight back, yellow-gray, the color of foam that floats to the top when you boil a chicken. A web of papery skin bunched up in tiny peaks on the backs of his hands.

Reynolds was seeing himself, where he'd be twenty-five years on down the line—if good bourbon didn't kill him first. Only difference, his daddy was a Medium, Reynolds an Xtra Large.

"Just hold on while I talk to Mama," Reynolds said. "But sure, I'll run out to the marina with you. Need to be back at the store by 12:00." Joy had agreed to open up for Reynolds at 10:00, but swore she would shut the liquor store down if Reynolds hadn't brought her a barbecue sandwich from Smokey's by noon.

Dottie Hairston was next to the side-yard fence when Reynolds moved by. "I knew you'd be too late. I told you to come when I called you. But what did I expect? You never did mind anyway. Not me, and not your mama."

"Sure is gonna be a lot more sunshine back there, Dottie," Reynolds said. He moved around the corner of the house. The backyard looked as if a twister had struck, a half-dozen trees felled across the yard. Willy Elmer wrestled with the chain saw that had jammed half way through tree number seven, the last one standing.

Edwina sat on the wooden steps that led down into the yard from the kitchen. Her arthritis kept getting more severe, and she wore baggy pants that hid her swollen knees.

Her arms sagged with folds of loose flesh. When she saw Reynolds it took an effort for her to turn towards him. She had a funny look on her face, as if she were trying to figure out where she was or what that old black man with a chain saw was doing in her back yard. For a moment Reynolds thought she didn't recognize him.

Reynolds eased down beside Edwina and she moved her hand as if to pat his knee. Instead, she pointed toward the back of the lot. "See those tomatoes?"

Reynolds nodded, gazed out to where a few orange tomatoes hung heavily from almost bare vines.

Edwina lowered her voice to a loud whisper. Reynolds mostly read her lips, her words lost in the roar from Willy Elmer's chain saw. "Good thing I switched them this summer. The heat's dried up most folks' vines." She fluttered her eyelids shut when she talked in confidence this way.

Reynolds was somewhere between puzzled and not giving a damn, right now mostly fascinated by the blue veins that roadmapped across his mama's closed eyelids. But his curiosity got to him. "Switched them with what?" he asked. "Some new Aggie variety?"

"No, son, I switched them." Edwina looked disgusted, as if she were trying to figure out how she had raised such an ignorant boy. "Switched them with a sumac limb. A nice, limber one." Edwina whipped the air with an imaginary sumac switch. "You lose some leaves, a bunch of blossoms, but those that survive that switching. . . ." she fluttered her eyes shut once again, "they make some tomatoes."

Edwina's eyes popped open again, as if she had gone off on a secret trip somewhere and just come back. "Did Sheila come with you? Where are those grandsons of mine? You never do bring Larry and Garry around anymore."

Before Reynolds could answer, try to explain once more that Sheila and the boys were out in Odessa, had been there for years, Edwina waved her arm around, taking in the backyard of butchered trees. "Everything was always falling. If it wasn't pecans, it was pecan hulls, or pecan leaves or pecan branches or those nasty strings of pollen." She gave a big sigh. "Pecan trees are nothing but trash, staining the walk, leaves choking up my flower beds, clogging up the gutters."

Edwina lowered her voice, fluttered her eyelids closed, drawing Reynolds back close. "Your daddy, he wouldn't rake a leaf, pick up a pecan. So I told him I would take care of the problem. For him not to worry—as if he ever did." Edwina fluttered her eyes back open again, a hint of a smile across her pale lips. "And see," she waved her bony arm across the destruction of the yard, "I did what I said. I took care of the problem."

Reynolds snorted a laugh and nodded. Edwina probably was a little daft by now, but his mama's peculiar craziness didn't bother him. There is some comfort in knowing that your own tendencies toward foul territory might be genetic, legitimately residing outside the ballpark where the big game is played.

But Reynolds could see, too, why his daddy might be taking off. Edwina's eccentricities could be amusing from a distance, but to dance with her unpredictability every day would be another matter.

"Daddy's leaving for a while," Reynolds said. "Will you be okay?"

"He's an old fool, messing with that machine." Edwina turned to Reynolds, aimed the part in the center of her hair straight at Reynolds' throat. Her eyes fluttered shut. "I'll be better off with him gone." She sighed. "Perpetual motion my eye. Nothing on earth is perpetual. He should know that. Only the Lord God will last forever. Your daddy, he'll think perpetual, wish he'd never heard the word when he winds up in hell with the devil."

Edwina opened her eyes. Reynolds had seen that look before, sad and pitiful, setting him up for the big question, the only one that seemed to matter to his mama. The "when are you coming back to the church?" question that he knew was always on Edwina's mind. A kinder question than the "when are you going to stop living in sin?" question she had tried more than once before.

Reynolds cut her off with a peck on the cheek, picked up the aroma of homemade biscuits and lavender face cream. He eased himself up from the steps. "Give me a call, Mama, if you need anything. I'll stop by."

"Perry's closer," she said. "He works too hard, though. Teaching nowadays is such a thankless job. But he stops by for me every Sunday morning. Sunday nights, too." Edwina fluttered her eyes closed. "I don't go to Wednesday night prayer meeting, though." Edwina poked her finger through the air to emphasize her point. "Wednesday. That's one word you won't find in the Bible." She shook her head.

"Wednesday. Wednesday. Wednesday. It sounds funny. Not

like a Bible word at all. I told that new preacher that he ought not to preach about Wednesday night prayer meeting at all. Whoever said anything in the Bible, I asked him, about the fourth day of the week being special. It's a silly idea." Edwina smirked, the same expression she got when an official signed White House letter came from President Clinton, responding to her several pages of advice. "That preacher boy, he didn't know what to say." She sighed again. "But Perry goes to prayer meeting, anyway. And I don't say a word about it." Edwina opened her eyes. "Perry's such a good boy."

Reynolds watched Willy Elmer back up a couple of steps, holding the chainsaw out to one side, while the last pecan tree fell. "Well, shit," Reynolds muttered to himself, and without looking back moved quickly around to the driveway where his daddy waited.

Reynolds drove his daddy's pickup through Cottonwood, past the new string of stores that had sprung up out along the highway that led to Dallas. While Reynolds drove Ray Senior pointed out the sights. There was "Bill's Dollar Store" and the "Buck and No More Store" and the "Way 2 Cheap Store." They passed the acres of junk cars in front of the A-1 Salvage Car Parts. A hand-painted sign across the galvanized metal front of the building boldly proclaimed, "Ain't God Great!"

They passed the Countywide Ford dealership and Ray Senior lifted his hand and nodded to no one in particular, maybe to the long row of shiny pickups that lined the road or to the strings of colored banners that seemed to wave back. "You going to miss being there?" Reynolds asked.

His daddy shook his head. The end of his cigarette flared when he lit it. He cracked the window on his side and the smoke trailed up and over his shoulder. "Something more important to do. And not a whole lot of time to do it."

Reynolds wanted to ask his daddy why in the hell he had stayed at the dealership all those years, peddling Ford pickups. Ray Senior should have been an engineer. Something else. Anything else.

"That place made me a good living," Ray Senior said, his voice dreamlike, as if he had somehow tuned in to his son's thoughts. "Not a bad living at all." He nodded as if to confirm the idea. "Got you boys through college, had some time to fish, made some good friends. A lot of loyal customers. You sell pickups to the same man for thirty years—six, seven, maybe even ten Ford pickups—you know you're doing something right." Ray Senior fished a black comb out of his back pocket, ran it slowly through the thinness of his hair. He leaned against the door, ducked down a little, trying to check his image in the outside mirror.

"I reckon so," Reynolds said, wondering if selling umpteen jillion six packs of Old Milwaukee over three years, much of it to the same dissipated beer drinkers, put him in that category of doing something right.

When they reached the first causeway that ran a quarter mile across a little neck of the lake, Ray Senior took a deep breath, followed by a rattling cough. "You know I don't believe in meddling in your affairs, son."

Oh, shit, Reynolds thought, having heard that line before, maybe said it more than once to Sheila or to his boys or even to Joy. What always followed had invariably amounted to piss-off ammunition for them all and hadn't changed things one iota. Maybe made them worse.

"Lake's a little choppy today," Reynolds said, ignoring his daddy, nodding out his window at the broken rows of whitecaps that skipped across the lake. The wind had picked up from the north and Reynolds gave a little shiver that caught him off guard. Ray Senior kept quiet and Reynolds knew his daddy intended to have his say, so he waited, giving Ray Senior room to keep going if he had to.

"Like I say, this is not meddling, but I don't want you to wind up like me, damned near seventy and all of a sudden surprised where the trail you took ended up." Ray Senior pointed ahead, held the end of his finger against the windshield for a minute, as if trying to touch some imaginary trail the Ford pickup was following. He pulled his finger back and waited while the smudge of his fingerprint began to fade. "What happens is this: You're somewhere back down the road a piece, maybe like you are now, maybe even younger. Probably married, living with a woman. Now that's the first mistake itself, but one I won't go into right now." He gave a little laugh, and Reynolds did, too.

"One day you're going about your business in a regular sort of a way and you turn, just a little, hardly enough to notice, and follow a new trail that forks off the one you were on. And for a few months, maybe even a few years, this new direction—one that looked easier, more inviting for whatever reasons—seems awfully close to the old trail. But what happens is this." Ray Senior held his hands up, the heels of his hands pressed together, his fingers held just a little apart. "Now back here," he explained, holding out his hands for Reynolds to see, "you can't see any difference. But it's started. By the time you get here," and he wiggled the ends of his fingers, "you've got off the trail a good piece. Of course, you can't go back and start over, and if you wait too long you'll get lost trying to cut across, the distance has got too wide." Ray Senior pulled his hands apart, held them there a minute, then reached into his pocket, fishing for something, but didn't pull anything out.

"You think I've got off the right trail, then? That's what you're saying?"

"I'm not saying right or wrong. What I might observe is that you're on a different trail than you once were on. Any damned fool can see that. I just thought I might say it out loud. You're young enough, I figure, to make some navigational corrections. But only if you have a mind to."

"What do you want? Me to be like Perry? Shit, Daddy, I do the best I can. I'm just different from Perry. Can you see me happy with a woman like Beth? And teaching a bunch of sullen adolescents why the government should work, but does only half-ass? To honor their politicos? No way."

Ray Senior frowned but didn't say a word, as if he was trying to hold something in.

"I can't be Perry," Reynolds said. "If that's what you and Mama want—well, that's too bad."

Ray shook his head. "Not Perry. Not in all the world would I want you to be like Perry." His voice got quiet then. "The last thing I need is another Perry."

Reynolds glanced over at his daddy, puzzled. "Mama thinks Perry walks on goddamn water," he said.

"Some things your mama doesn't know."

Reynolds waited, hoping his daddy might go on, but for a couple of miles they both got quiet, Reynolds bothered by his daddy's story of how you could stray off the trail without hardly knowing it. Shit, he thought, what are detour signs for? Road repairs ahead? Getting off the road of life and back on is what it's all about. Isn't it?

"I know where I'm headed," Reynolds finally said, his words tight in his mouth. But inside he knew that was a lie.

Right now he couldn't see much farther than the hood of his daddy's pickup, and then, when they cruised around the next bend, he could see the broadness of the lake and the Red Top Store and Marina.

The parking lot held a couple of pickups and an old Dodge with its hood up. Scraps of plastic whipped in the wind, trapped around its tires. A Blue Bell ice cream truck was pulled in sideways across the two handicap parking spaces. Reynolds eased the pickup in behind the truck and waited, the engine running. He turned the heater up a notch.

"Pull on around back," Ray Senior said, waving his hand in a circle. "Closer to my boat."

Reynolds eased the truck around the store and killed the engine. From there, near the rickety wooden dock, the two men watched the lake in silence. Reynolds was glad he didn't have to cross the lake against the whip of that fresh norther, but he wished his daddy would get on with it. He wished he'd kept quiet about Perry, felt like a teenager bringing that up. Spouting off like that never did Reynolds any good.

"Lake's a little rough," Reynolds observed.

"Not as rough as staying in town."

"Maybe not," Reynolds said. He didn't really want to know.

Then Ray Senior rolled his window all the way up, checked behind to see that they were alone. He turned towards Reynolds. "Now this is something not to be shared, not to go outside of this pickup. Strictly between you and me." Ray Senior gave Reynolds a look that was not questioning, but demanding.

Reynolds nodded. "Sure. No problem here."

"Okay," Ray Senior said. He got quiet for a moment. Then

he looked out over the lake while he spoke, as if he were talking to himself, saying something that he couldn't help but say. "Perry killed a man. It's been a long time ago now, and wasn't exactly deliberate. But he killed a young Marine when he was in the Philippines."

"No way," Reynolds said shaking his head. But he could feel the excitement swell up in him. A feeling of dread and a rise of pleasure at the same time. "I never heard that."

That time of Reynolds' life, when he was down in Austin at the university, when he had begun his tangle with Sheila, was mostly lost to him. For sure Reynolds stayed away from Cottonwood, and Perry was pretty much lost to Reynolds, putting in his three-year stint in the Marines. By the time Reynolds had relocated back up to Cottonwood with the bank, his little brother had finished up his degree over at East Texas State and married Beth. Next thing Reynolds knew Perry had settled into a teaching job at the local high school. Maybe not quite that clean and easy, as things turned out.

The story that Ray Senior told to his oldest son that day poured out in a quiet stream. Reynolds rolled his window down a little, letting in the lake smells of algae and dead fish and spilled fuel that all mixed with the crisp October air. Both men stared straight ahead while Ray spoke, the older man stopping only when a couple of cars and then a truck pulling a boat eased around the pea-gravel parking lot behind them.

Perry had killed a man in a bar, a Marine called Mouth by his buddies, just a boy from Stillwater, Oklahoma. A boy who went a little crazy when he drank, and that night he had by all accounts drunk a lot. Perry killed him, smashed him on the side of his head with a cue ball, and when Mouth hit the floor he still gripped a locked-open Buck knife in his right hand. Self-defense, everyone gathered there agreed, but Perry spent some weeks in the brig during the investigation, and slipped back into Cottonwood several months early with a dishonorable discharge from the Marine Corps.

Ray Senior had told no one, Edwina not enough attuned to the passage of time or military ways to question Perry's premature return.

"A lot to keep to yourself," Reynolds finally said after his daddy got quiet. "I guess Beth knows."

"That's Perry's business, who he might have told. But I imagine he shared that with her. I hope to hell so."

"Is this where all that church stuff comes from?" Reynolds asked.

"A man takes his comfort where he can," Ray Senior said. Then he gave a little laugh. A sad laugh, Reynolds thought. "Or he does without, gets along best he can."

"Why are you telling me this now?" Reynolds asked. "Why not years ago? How long has it been? Fifteen? Twenty years ago?"

"A couple of reasons, I guess. Perry's moved off to the side in a way, headed somewhere I'm not sure. Different from you. Has no patience with politics, you know." Ray Senior shook his head. "Hasn't filed with the IRS in five or six years. Can't disagree with that too much. But, I'm afraid he's going to spout off at school and lose himself a good teaching job. I thought you might be able to talk to him, tone him down a little."

"Not much chance of that," Reynolds said. "That's mostly B.S., a lot of town talk, don't you think? He just needs to mellow out a little."

"He's right near forty," Ray Senior said quietly. "He's got

a nice enough wife and a fine daughter. What does he need so that he'll mellow out?" Ray Senior sighed. "He just never learned to get along. And that Republic of Texas sort of stuff, militia this, militia that, all those gun magazines. It will lead to no good."

Ray Senior cracked his window again, pinched the ash end of his smoked-down cigarette between his thumb and finger, and flicked it away. He rolled the window back up, tight. "This is between us. Perry's on some kind of probation for teaching those screwball ideas of his."

Reynolds shrugged. He'd never seen Perry's right wing tendencies as a problem. Not much different from most of the yahoos in that part of East Texas, but he had always figured Perry for being more intelligent, a cut above.

Maybe Reynolds had been wrong. A long time ago he and Perry silently had agreed not to disagree, and that put politics and religion out of bounds. Along with sex and booze. Didn't leave much but the Cowboys and the Rangers, and Reynolds didn't give a damn about either one of them.

"You said you had a couple of reasons for telling me about Perry," Reynolds said. "Hoping I could talk to him. Well, I can't. Not yet. I hope you understand. What's the other reason?"

"Oh, the time seemed right, I guess," Ray said. "I figure you've been up and down enough yourself to understand it now. Maybe not when it happened. You know, back then all the answers might have seemed too easy."

"Sure not too easy now."

"Hard sometimes."

"Damned hard."

Finally Ray Senior made a move to leave. "You sure you want to go," Reynolds asked.

Ray Senior nodded. "Before the end," he said, "a man's got to give himself over to something he believes in. Even if it's wrongheaded, even if it may never work." He jerked his thumb back over his shoulder towards the tarp-shrouded perpetual motion machine behind him.

It got quiet in the pickup then, the only sound the wind that whipped by in gusts, the only movement the gentle rocking of the two men as they swayed together in the safety of the truck.

FOUR

R EYNOLDS ran his daddy's new pickup hard heading back into Cottonwood, but it was nearly 1:00 by the time he made it to the Ford dealer. There he wrangled a ride with Buddy Miller back to Edwina's where Reynolds had left his Lincoln Town Car. Reynolds knew that by now Joy would be starved and pissed and might even be gone. Reynolds could picture Joy racing off in her Dodge Dart for a hamburger while dozens of thirsty Saturday fishermen peered in the windows, cussing his locked-tight liquor store.

So when Buddy pulled up in front of Edwina's, Reynolds slid out of the pickup and quickly slipped away. As he drove off the chain saw still sputtered and roared in his mama's back yard, and he figured Willy Elmer had about buzzed the pecan trees into a cord of firewood.

Reynolds did take the time to swing in the drive-through at Smokey's BBQ on his way back though town. He waited, lined up behind a couple of pickups, his Lincoln idling roughly. Reynolds felt antsy, unsettled. He flipped on the radio, punched it to the one Dallas station he liked. Organ music. Bach, he figured, in his high church mood. He turned the volume low, tried to relax, calm down a little, but the music crowded him, clamored and strained and raced up and down until Reynolds finally snapped the radio silent. He drummed his fingers on the steering wheel and finally edged his car forward to the service window.

A bored voice crackled over the speaker and Reynolds ordered a couple of chopped beef sandwiches. Not even a "Thank you" from the kid. "Boy," Reynolds wanted to say, "you'd be out of here if this was still a bank and I was still in charge."

"Yeah, Reynolds," he said, talking out loud to himself. "You sure are some big fucking deal."

Reynolds no longer felt embarrassed to stop by the bank-building-cum-barbecue joint where he, not all that long ago, had been the top dog, numero uno, presidente, and wait while a chalky-faced teenager tossed the sandwiches in the bank's old slide-out and pop-open drive-through window where Reynolds could reach them. But he still didn't have the heart to go inside, tackle a plate of barbecue with a plastic fork on a plastic plate with that enormous vault staring at him from the back of the room. A joke, some comment by Smokey about the way things used to be would set him off, he knew, and that was one situation he could avoid.

On the way back out to Lake City he lost himself in Perry's story, puzzled by what that killing might mean, how his history with Perry might spin around in light of this disclosure. So the good brother had killed a man. He might not be so good after all. Reynolds had a lot of revision to do—now he saw that he didn't really know Perry at all. How this would change things he wasn't sure. And what kind of trouble Perry might be headed toward he couldn't guess.

But Ray Senior was no dummy. He might be a Ford truck salesman, but he was a good one. And one trait of a good salesman was knowing how much to disclose. More deals had been blown, his daddy liked to tell him, by talking too much, not knowing when to stop. Reynolds wished his daddy had gone just a little farther about Perry's fall. Maybe next time. Or maybe Perry would give him some opening. If he ever saw him.

When Reynolds pulled in beside the liquor store the "Yep" sign hung tilted in the window, good news he figured, but no guarantee the place was open, or that Joy would be there. Then he spotted Joy's car in its usual place and knew everything would be okay, that he'd have to take a little crap from her for running late, but after a couple of bites of Smokey's barbecue she would settle down.

On the opposite side of the store, pulled in under the overhang of a stunted elm tree, Reynolds noticed a Chevy Bel Air that belonged to Stick, one of Reynolds' regulars, a fellow Reynolds went to high school with—until Stick dropped out. Stick never parked out front like a regular customer, but always to the side under the shade of the tree. At first Reynolds thought he parked out there because he felt inferior in some way, not good enough to park smack dab in the middle of the Lake City Liquor Store parking lot. But finally Reynolds decided it wasn't that at all, only that Stick felt special, as if he could take the only shade around and protect his Chevy's paint job, keep it from fading in the Texas sun.

Stick was as good as a customer could be, drinking both plenty and regularly. He stopped by every Saturday, and slapped his cash on the counter when he came in the door. The cash on the counter was Stick's up front money, his earnest money, so to speak, guaranteeing that this would be a good-faith transaction, that he was not just one of those cruise-through customers who study all the wine labels and leave. No, the cash on the counter was a deposit and reflected the integrity of Stick's life, his place in the scheme of things as a serious beer-buying customer. That way he could take his time and shop thoughtfully, although he always ended up sliding a case of Lone Star across the counter.

Stick dropped by most Saturdays to stock up on enough beer to see him through the weekend. He had been called Stick since high school days, not because he was skinny as a stick (which he was), but because of the early promise he demonstrated with a cue stick in Cottonwood's only pool hall.

When Stick dropped out of high school at sixteen he took the only job he could get—one he still had—the worst job Reynolds could imagine. Stick drove a gut truck every other day to a glue factory east of Dallas, the truck packed full of animal waste from the meat packing plant outside of Cottonwood. The truck was easy to spot, with strands of cow intestines trailing along behind, whipping in the wind. Stick drove the truck, his head stuck out the open window like a cow dog, his face in the breeze. He wore goggles to keep the bugs out of his eyes.

Reynolds stopped in the open doorway and checked around. Sure enough Stick was inside the store, towards the back, watching the beer cooler like it was a TV. He wore a pair of overalls that was smeared with grease. Joy was no-where in sight.

"Hey, Stick," Reynolds said in his best good old boy way. He lifted the white sack of barbecue sandwiches in greeting. "Que pasa? Been working on your truck?"

Stick turned. He never looked surprised, but—in an odd way—wise. Reynolds figured it was his flat top, his hair still cut the same as twenty years before and butch waxed in place. Except now there wasn't much hair in the center, and what there was stuck up on either side like owl ears.

"Hey, old buddy. Nada happenin'. For damn sure nada." Then Stick checked his grease-smeared overalls. "Need to do some wash, I guess." He reached in his pocket, pulled out a wad of bills, proud all over his face. "Sold a little beer for you, a little cheap whiskey."

"Where the hell is Joy?" Reynolds asked, trying to keep the annoyance out of his voice. "Did you ring those sales up? She show you how to operate that cash register?"

"Didn't see no need for that. Joy, she went out back. To the trailer, I guess. She was about to pass out the way she looked. Said she had to find something to eat. For her and that girl of hers."

"What do you mean, 'that girl of hers?'" And then Reynolds knew. "Oh, shit." It was Deanie, he guessed. But what in the hell was she doing here? A pickup pulling a boat circled out front and stopped. A couple of fellows piled out of the cab.

"That's a crock a shit," one of them hollered.

"You can bet your mama's sweet ass it's not," the other one said with a grin.

"You watch the store a couple of minutes more?" Reynolds asked.

Stick got a satisfied look on his face and nodded. "Whatever, good buddy. You want me to work the machine?" Now he looked worried.

"Just hang on to the cash," Reynolds said, and he headed for the back door. "I won't be long."

Joy didn't look up when Reynolds stepped into the trailer. She sat at the little fold-down dinette table, a scattering of cellophane wrappers everywhere, a stack of Tom's peanut butter-and-cheese crackers towering next to a carton of milk.

Reynolds looked around for Deanie, then heard a flush from the bathroom. "Company, huh," Reynolds grunted.

"You're late," Joy said. "I would have closed you down if Stick hadn't come along."

"Stick always comes along. Your mama drop Deanie by?"

"Don't just stand there holding the sack." Joy reached her hand out, a quick, angry gesture.

Reynolds tossed it on the table, and the tower of peanut butter-and-cheese crackers toppled to the side.

"Shitass," Joy said.

"Mama was sick," Reynolds said, thinking fast. Joy was a sucker for old folks who were sick.

Joy looked up towards him for the first time, stared somewhere over his shoulder. She had worry all over her face. "Bad sick?"

"Hurt, actually. A tree limb hit her when it fell, thought it might have broke her arm. But it didn't. Made her sick, though. I stayed around extra. For Mama." The good son, Reynolds thought. He shook his head. The good liar, anyway.

The bathroom door squeaked open, and Deanie went straight to the TV, flipped the channel, and moved to the end of the bed. Sounded like figure-skating competition to Reynolds. He hated figure skating. It wasn't a real sport.

"Turn it down, honey," Joy said.

Deanie didn't move. "There's no remote."

"It's an old TV, hon." Joy's words bit into the stale air. "Turn it down. Now."

Deanie dragged herself to the TV, wagging side to side as she walked. Her straight brown hair swayed; a perfect, practiced pout on her lips. She turned the volume down an indiscernible fraction.

"More."

Deanie gave a big sigh. She turned the volume down and plopped back across the bed.

Reynolds pulled a chair around, straddled it backwards and started in on one of the sandwiches.

Joy took a bite, shook her head in disgust and stuck her sandwich in the microwave on the cabinet behind her.

"That'll make it tough," Reynolds warned while he chewed.

"Life's tough," Joy snapped.

"Hand me a beer, will you?" Reynolds asked.

"You know where they are," Joy said, peering into the microwave. But she got Reynolds a Shiner Bock, slid it across the table to him.

"Deanie. Is she staying long?" Reynolds asked, nodding his head to the back of the trailer.

Joy sat back down with the sandwich. Unwrapped it. Steam went everywhere.

"Gonna be tough now." Reynolds said.

"Least of my problems." Joy licked her fingers. She softened a little; Reynolds could feel the softness float towards him through the air and didn't know if she would cry or smile. Either Joy needed something, Reynolds knew, or was going to break some bad news to him. He hoped she wasn't going to leave. Not yet.

"My mama's taken a job," she said, "the night shift at some nursing home. I tried to talk her out of it, but she's broke. Bo Reed—that old fellow who lives with her—he's got cancer

of the lungs. They took him off to a specialist, a smart doctor, but he says there's nothing to do. Can't cut it out without deflating the lungs, I guess. So Bo's going to Ciudad
Acuna. Mexico has a new cure down there. Works every time
they say." Joy stopped for a minute. "Do you believe that? I
think they'll just take his dollars. He'll be broke and dead in
three months. Mama, she should have married him years ago.
She'd have some claim now on his social security."

"What about Deanie, then?" Reynolds had finished off his
barbecue sandwich and started in on a package of cheese
crackers.

"Can you imagine, sixty-two and single, a job wiping up
after old folks eight hours a day. Not for me. I'm going to get
fixed in life. Have a real job, with benefits, do it all myself."

"Good luck. darlin'. It's not all that easy you know."

"Is if you get prepared. Get a certificate." She looked over
at Reynolds. "If you don't wait too late to start."

"It would be a shame to take Deanie out of her school up
there now," Reynolds said. "Maybe after Christmas would be
okay, but right in the middle of the term? I don't know."

"I'll move out then. Find a place of my own. For me and
Deanie." Joy leaned across the table, looking Reynolds right
in the eye. She leaned over, touched Reynolds' arm. He
caught a glimpse of the top of her bra, the rise of her breasts.
Reynolds, he thought, you're a weak son of a bitch.

"It's Saturday," Reynolds said. He swallowed hard, took a
long sip of beer. "We've got a couple of days to figure this
out. A few days wouldn't matter, you know, but this place
just wasn't meant for a . . .a . . ." and he almost said "family."
That scared the shit out of him. "It's too small for more
than one or two. You know that."

"Deanie's awful little, though," Joy said. "She'd fit on the
couch."

Reynolds pushed himself up out of the chair, checked the clock above the stove.

"Hey, I've got to get back to the store. Stick doesn't know refries about that register. He screws it up, the state boys'll be on me like brown on a cow pattie." Reynolds stood up, turned the chair back around with his boot, and shoved it against the table.

"Hi, Deanie. Bye, Deanie." Reynolds waved toward the back.

"Oooh, cool," Deanie said, her eyes never leaving the TV. "Mama, you should see this."

It took half an hour for Stick to count out the money for Reynolds. He lined up the cash in four stacks on the counter— one for beer, one for wine, one for the hard stuff, and a miscellaneous pile for a jar of stink bait and a couple of treble-hook spinners.

Reynolds gave Stick his weekly case of Lone Star for helping out. "Free gratis?" Stick asked. "Better than the lottery around here. You ever decide to sell out, let me know first." Stick patted the case of beer that rested on his shoulder. He wagged his head side to side. "Man, do you ever have it made. A good lookin' woman, living next to your own store crammed full of booze. What a deal."

"Yeah, Stick," Reynolds said. "I've damned sure got it made."

FIVE

WHEN HIS pager buzzed, Perry had just finished giving the blessing for Sunday dinner.
At that moment Edwina turned her chair to
the side and pushed herself up. She steadied herself and waddled back to the kitchen to check on the gravy that sim-
mered on the stove. Perry checked the pager on his belt and
mentally noted the number; then he glanced around
Edwina's dining room. Perry sat uncomfortably at the foot of
the table, in the dimness of Edwina's small dining room.
From there he could look out the window to his left and see
into the bright, treeless backyard. Straight ahead was the
kitchen where his mother now fussed around the stove, and
to his right, past Beth and through a doorless opening, he
could see into the living room, a straight line to the television set, that room's focal point. The television was on, its
sound turned down, and some all-terrain vehicle miracu-
lously made its way up a steep mountainside while the Dallas
Cowboys took a break from the Sunday action.

Perry sat in one of five matching straight-back oak chairs

grouped around the rectangular table. On Sundays Edwina went all out and covered the table with an unimaginably intricate tablecloth that her mother had crocheted and pieced sometime around the turn of the century. The cloth had yellowed in a place or two where it had been creased and folded and stored, but was still a magnificent handiwork, whether a tribute to the skill and perseverance of Perry's grandmother or to her blind desperation and boredom no one knew, or said.

Jennifer sat immediately to Perry's left, slouched down in her chair, trapped between him and Edwina whose regular place was next to her, in the chair nearest the kitchen. Beth, on his right, up until now had been back and forth to the kitchen that Perry faced. Beth seemed eager to help, and managed to keep the small talk going with Edwina, who alternated between her running complaint about the lack of fresh chickens at the Buddy's Supermarket in town and the shoddy sales items at the local Bealls.

Perry didn't know how Beth did it, kept up that cheerful patter of talk. On the one hand Perry wished she could be more honest and straightforward, but on the other hand, maybe it was better this way. Smoothing things over was a trait of Beth's that worked in his best interest. Not a trait to disparage at all.

When Perry had glanced down, responding to the beep of the pager, Beth ignored it, but a determined look slid across her face. Perry hoped the look reflected her determination to ignore his odd, unexplained phone calls, and not her resolve to force the truth from him, regardless of the cost.

The family, this part of it anyway, gathered here in Edwina's house every Sunday. It was now just the four of them, Perry and Beth and Jennie stopping by earlier in the morning for Edwina, the four of them riding to church in Beth's three-year old van. The four of them then lined up on a pew near the rear of that little church they attended faithfully. Numbers were of no importance. "Where two or three are gathered together. . . ." and so on. Brother Johnson pounded his fist against the bible he clutched in his left hand as he assigned to hell the sinners of the world who lived outside the flock.

"Outside the flock," also described the in-limbo and for-now-lost status accorded to the absent Ray Senior, his chair directly opposite Perry at the head of the table, the chair tipped forward, leaning gently against the softness of the crocheted cloth. It was significant—to Edwina, at least—that Ray Senior's chair remained there, ready to be tipped back upright on all four of its sturdy legs when finally her wayward husband repented and crawled back home.

No limbo status, no tipped-toward-the-table chair for Reynolds, however. The place for the sixth chair—it would have fit to Perry's right, next to Beth—was vacant, an empty space. The lost son and brother was so far estranged from the family rectangle that his chair had been removed from the dining room altogether and now sat upright against a wall in Edwina's bedroom, its cane seat piled with stacks of quilt pieces and folds of tissue paper patterns.

Ray Senior and Reynolds resided in different spheres of absentia, but the same rules applied to both, their names off limits, their ghosts in the room never acknowledged, as if they had never shared the house or the Sunday dinner table at all.

Reynolds did come and go; he stopped by his mama's now and then for a quick visit. He crashed occasionally in his and Perry's old bedroom when he felt too unsteady for the drive back out from town to his trailer or was in the turmoil of a breakup or breakdown of some female entanglement. But Reynolds was off limits, especially on Sundays, since he both owned a liquor store and, as Edwina quoted from a true gospel tract she waved at him off and on, had "lived with a woman outside the sanctity of marriage." Edwina always made her oldest son pay, getting her sermonettes in over the rare breakfasts she shared with her mostly hangdog and hungover oldest son.

Perry found it easier to go through the motions. His Sunday performance might be mostly a charade, but it served his needs. Perry liked, he actually needed, the sense of order he found in church, the simplicity of its truth similar to what he had once found and then lost in the Marines. The church, at least, had rules, gave structure to his relationship with Beth, and would give Jennie something to fall back on through her teenaged years. There was an overlay, as it turned out, a reciprocity between Perry's political ideas and the surety of the church's beliefs. A reassurance that the truth does exist and that it can be discovered and embraced, even outside the misguided mainstream of the world.

Besides, with Ray Senior no longer around for Sunday dinners, Perry had a clear view of the Cowboys on the TV in the front room. He glanced back and forth, between plays and during timeouts nodding while Edwina carried on with her stories, told over and over, agreeing with her moral conclusions, raising the tone of his voice when Jennie slouched at the table or acted disrespectfully to Edwina or otherwise got out of line.

After Perry's prayer, with the gravy now hot and being ladled around, Edwina jumped right into eye shadow, worried that Jennifer at fourteen might not understand fully the underlying messages sent by the green wash she had brushed over each eyelid.

"Now, a little pink lipstick is acceptable for a girl your age, and maybe just a touch of color to your cheeks, but not eye shadow. That's for show girls, movie stars, and such. You agree don't you, Perry?"

Perry looked at Edwina, tried to picture her ever as a girl of fourteen, noticed her lightly touched lips, the pale blush of rouge on cheeks that drooped like the wallpaper above her.

"These days I hardly know what to think," Perry said. "But yes, Mama, there is some wisdom in what you say. What we truly are, our essence you might say, resides inside ourselves, and often all the fashion folderol is just a way to keep it buried." He didn't want to screw with this now, the Cowboys were playing at Washington, always a tough game, and there was the message on his beeper. Skinny and Fat Hand and Shadow wanted something.

"We all go through stages," Beth said. "I can remember being a girl, wanting to do what was popular."

"Mini skirts were popular," Edwina said, patting her lips with a linen napkin, then checking it for stains. "But popular has nothing to do with being decent."

In the living room the Cowboys were backed up to their own fifteen. Third and acres, they called time out. Perry reengaged. "I'll tell you what, though, I think this is one fine spread. Let's dig in."

"Well," Edwina said, "I know what to think. The answer is there, right in the bible, if only we search for it. Seek and ye shall find. Have some roast chicken, hon." She forked a chicken thigh onto Jennie's plate.

Jennie frowned, rolled her eyes. Just like her mother, Perry thought.

"Mama," Perry pointed his fork at Jennie's plate, "she likes white meat. If there is some."

"Certainly there is some. Even these days a hen has dark meat and white meat. Some things never change."

Edwina went all out for Sunday after church dinners, got up at 5:00 to start the yeast rolls, made the dressing, boiled the potatoes, put the hen in the oven. It was all cooked, sitting out on top of Edwina's stove when they came in after church. She only had to heat up the brown gravy.

"I don't know how you do all of this," Beth always said.

Later, in the car going home, Beth swore they would get botulism some day from the way Edwina left everything out while they were at church. "You'd think she didn't know what a refrigerator was for. I could smell something a little off today. Not ruined, but a little off."

"It's worked for the past fifty years," Perry said.

"I'm not going next week," Jennifer said from the back seat. "I swear I'm not. Not unless you tell Grandma to leave me alone. Not to Grandma's and not to church either."

"Now your grandmother is one thing," Perry said, "and she has her ways—not that they're all wrong, either. But the Lord is another, and if I were you young lady," he eyed Jennie in the van's rearview mirror, "I'd be a little more careful speaking of Christ and His church."

Jennie slouched down in the back seat. She was a pretty girl, lucky in some ways, getting Beth's long legs and curls of dark hair, but she would have to watch her weight. Perry would talk to her about that. Sometime when they could be alone. Or he would get Beth to do it. A daughter isn't all that easy.

Perry loosened his tie and unbuttoned the top button of his soft yellow shirt. He nodded and waved at the cars they passed as he drove through town. Perry sat up high in the van. He felt good in Cottonwood on days like this, when he had been to church and had a fine meal at his mama's house and then knew almost everyone in every car he met on the way back home.

The downside in a small town is that you have to watch your step, but for Perry that wasn't a problem. He didn't drink or smoke or shoot pool with the trash at the beer joints out past Lake City. He'd back off a little at school, maybe write a letter to the superintendent, explaining that much of what he said in class was just a ploy to stimulate creative analysis, that he simply hadn't gotten to the part of the lesson plan where he explained to his students that his political theories had been an invention, contrived solely to judge their reactions, and so on, and so on. He would think up some bullshit that would get the old fart off his back for a while.

This gun thing he'd better watch, though. That could get out of hand. But you had to be smart, and Perry was; he knew when to go for it, when to pull back. That call on his beeper was probably to set up the next delivery. Perry would be a little more assertive when he called back, try to make things happen on his terms. Maybe he would let it drop that he had killed a Lance Corporal in the Marines. They might realize then that he could be a major player, if he just wanted to be. Or maybe he would keep quiet. That fight with Mouth had best remain his secret. His and Beth's and Ray Senior's.

Perry pulled the van into the driveway, and stopped under the carport. This house would be his, paid off in no time at all with the gun trading money he was picking up. An extra house payment here, another there. They really added up. The house had a nice ranch-style plan, with mottled brick all the way across the front, and wood planking in the back and down both sides. Three bedrooms, two baths, clean white walls, built-ins, the whole works, and on a couple of acres, to boot. Built on the best lot in Boswell's Ranchettes, with restrictions and its own water system. Flat sandy land where you could have a garden if you wanted, plant a few fruit trees. Perry had started some Brazos blackberry vines on the back fence and they would be full of berries by next summer.

All in all, Perry acknowledged, a good enough life could be had here. A stretch above what Ray Senior had achieved, for sure. And light years better than Reynolds, after the oil price collapse had knocked him down more than a few notches.

Yeah, a couple of more shipments and Perry might back off. His recruits, except for Snider, had turned out to a bunch of losers, in and out of trouble, lacking the moral starch to be reliable when the time came. Perry might just sell out the whole inventory, give Snider his share, and close the operation down. If things got messy it might affect Jennie's future and his and Beth's security. Perry's dishonorable discharge from the Marines had cut off pension possibilities, but his teaching retirement would be fully vested if he hung on another seven years. Perry was, in his gut, a man of principle, but he was wise to the old axiom that cautioned, "choose your battles wisely."

Jennie was out of the car and into the house in a moment. Perry reached back for his suit coat and Beth touched his arm. "Who called?" she asked.

"Oh, it's not really important. Some possibilities I'm working on, everything still up in the air."

Beth pulled her hand back and sighed.

"Look, I'll tell you if anything of consequence develops. I've told you that. But right now it's my business. I don't have to know every detail of your life, do I?"

"No, but this is different."

"How can you say it's different if you don't know what it is?"

"You can tell me."

"And I will. When the time is right, I promise I will."

Beth frowned. She shook her head and stepped quickly down from the van.

Perry moved towards his pickup. "I'll be right back," he said. But Beth already had disappeared inside the house.

SIX

FROM the table in Edwina's dining room Beth had stared straight ahead and into the backyard, now sparkling in the November light of this crisp Sunday noon. With the pecan trees gone the place had lifted, lightened in a way, and Beth understood Edwina's need to hack away at whatever caused the gloom.

Edwina had placed plastic terra cotta saucers on each of the tree stumps back there, filling them alternately with water and bird seed, and now a couple of blue jays fussed, fluttering above one of the saucers. Nearby, in the shade cast by another saucer, a longhaired white cat rested, nonchalantly licking the top of one paw.

Edwina was still puttering in the kitchen, heating the gravy in a saucepan on top of the stove. Perry caught Beth's eye, nodded towards the kitchen, and Beth felt herself frown, then she slid her chair back, and turned towards the kitchen. "Edwina," she said, her voice light, pleasant, and forced, "do you need some help out there?"

Beth knew that Perry wished she would go in there and

help out, but Beth had been doing this for almost seventeen years, and by now she knew that Edwina would just shoo her back out.

Beth looked around. This house was falling apart. The wallpaper sagged from the ceiling in the front room, and brown water spots circled the paper over her head. The floor between the kitchen and dining room gave when she walked across it, the pine boards soft, and she was afraid that one day they would collapse with Edwina, especially the way she had put on weight.

"Termites," she had told Perry. "I'll bet anything her house is eaten up by termites."

But Perry dismissed Beth—she should be used to it by now. "It's always been that way," he said.

Always? Always? When Ray Senior and Edwina built this house in 1952 those boards were rotten? That's what she wanted to say to Perry, but she didn't.

Beth kept her eyes open while Perry gave the blessing. She watched Edwina's eyes fluttering shut, watched Jennie, lost somewhere outside the prayer, outside the room, outside the house. In another world, Beth knew. And she didn't blame her. Perry the prayer-maker, pious, self-righteous. Perry the angry ex-Marine, the resentful teacher, the zealously cynical citizen. There were so many Perrys, Beth wasn't sure she knew any of them, anymore.

Then, as if Perry's somber "Amen" had caused it, the pager he always wore on his belt went off, an irritating beep that he quickly silenced, a beep that Edwina ignored. Why was Beth the only one to think it strange that a schoolteacher would wear a pager? On Sunday? She gave Perry her look, the "I don't like what I see happening" look, but Perry ignored her. The same way he and Edwina ignored the empty chair at the head of the table where Ray Senior had always sat.

Beth missed her father-in-law, the way he injected a little humor into this weekly gathering, refusing to take it all quite so seriously. He used to drive Edwina to church Sunday mornings, maybe even get up early to wipe down the pickup's chrome, and Windex the windshield. Those Sundays he sat beside her, arms folded across his chest, nodding off during the sermon. Later, outside, while the flock milled around in front of the church, Ray Senior bummed cigarettes from his old buddies, his back turned to "Madam Queen" while he furtively smoked and expounded eloquently on the new F-150s that Ford had come out with.

Reynolds' chair had been removed completely, and Beth wasn't all that sure that doing so was a mistake, for Reynolds had demonstrated his unrepentant wildness. But now, as she thought about it, watching Perry correct Jennie across the way, watching the quickness of his eyes as he glanced back and forth towards the turned-down TV in the front room, watching Edwina's approval of her younger son, maybe Reynolds was simply the honest one. The first time that thought had occurred to her.

Edwina pushed the gravy boat her way, that brown essence of roast chicken. She shook her head, passed it on to Perry, who was still nodding while Edwina went on about Jennie's eye shadow. Does he have to be a know-it-all, an expert on everything, for God's sake? Even eye shadow?

Beth eyed the gravy again. Oh, why not, she said to herself, and then remembered her aerobics instructor, the way before each class she repeated little homilies of encouragement. Silly little sayings for the most part, as if that strip-center room, with its Astroturf floor and acoustical tile ceiling and mirrors all along one wall was a kindergarten and not filled with all shapes of grown women. But one saying Beth remembered: "Weight is simply a blend of unhappiness and boredom and food."

So far Beth had lost the fight against too much food, but at that moment she recognized the enemy for the first time, and it wasn't food at all, but unhappiness and boredom. Saying "no" to the gravy was easier if she felt she could say "yes" to herself. Things would have to change, between her and Perry, between her and the rest of Cottonwood. She would have to go outside of him, maybe quit her job at the county clerk's office. Maybe she could get on as a decorating consultant at the new Lack's Furniture out in Cottonwood Plaza. She had a flair, her friends told her, with her house. She really didn't care—it would be a way out into the world, a way for her to have something besides a terminally boring job.

This extra money that Perry dropped her way from time to time was some bizarre form of blackmail, she now realized, hush money. She was losing Perry, maybe already had lost him. It was as if his secret he had brought home from the Marines had bound them together for so many years that it had become a prison for them both. Now his midnight boat rides, his secretive phone calls, the reprimand from the school superintendent, the unexplained stacks of extra twenty dollar bills he left on the kitchen counter for her to have—all of this began to add up for Beth. It almost made sense, formed a pattern, but one that she couldn't quite put together.

She needed someone to talk to, and she thought about Reynolds, now after her new assessment of his honesty, wondering if he would have some insight into Perry that she was too close to see. Reynolds certainly wasn't naive. But Perry would never forgive her for going to him, and she wasn't sure Reynolds would take her seriously. He was so unpredictable, especially when he drank.

No, she would get help from somewhere else, and right then, while Perry furtively watched the Cowboys on the screen in the next room, while Edwina went on in her stupid way about chickens nowadays having white meat and dark meat, and while Jennie sulked with "run-away" written all over her face and deep in her eyes, Beth knew what she had to do.

⊠ ⊠ ⊠

The next morning, Beth stood at the living room window of her house, pulled the curtain back just a little and watched Perry pull his pickup down the driveway, headed for school. She could tell by the way he moved his head back and forth that he was lecturing Jennie about something, and she could tell from the way Jennie hugged the door on her side of the truck that she had pulled her coat around her tightly to shut him out. She had wrapped herself in the unhappy comfort of her own secret world.

"This can't go on," Beth said aloud and moved back to the kitchen, where the smell of bacon still hung in the air. She had an hour before she went to work, so now she moved quickly to the built-in desk at one end of the room. From there she could see into the backyard where the new white picket fence enclosed the concrete patio. It was crowded with its pots of cut-back geraniums and yellow-green paddles of prickly pear starts.

Beth watched the new neighbor in the house behind theirs, a woman—hardly more than a girl, she appeared—

who hung a long line of diapers in the morning sun. This new family had moved in only last week, but already yellow and red plastic toys surrounded a pile of builder's sand in the backyard. She and her husband were from Dallas, Beth had heard. He was the manager of the new Jiffy Lube out east of town.

Perry suggested that Beth bake something to take over, to be neighborly, but the lots out there in Boswell's Ranchettes were so deep, that Beth didn't feel all that close, that neighborly. But maybe she would bake some oatmeal cookies to take over later and keep a few around for Jennie. If Perry hadn't suggested it, she probably would have already.

Beth pulled the phone book down from the shelf and found the number she wanted. She really should run into Piggly Wiggly this morning early. She would have time to hurry back and put something in her slow cooker for dinner, and for a moment she almost hung up the receiver. But she dialed, and in a moment a woman answered, "Shawnee County Sheriff's office. How can I help you?" Beth asked for Bobby Ray Warren. The woman put her on hold and the local radio station came on, ads for the new Ford pickups at Countywide Ford, where Ray Senior no longer worked. Beth felt sad, a little shocked even, with the realization that life did go on, that like Ray Senior, you could give twenty or thirty or forty years of your life to something like the Ford dealership—or to someone—and when you were gone nothing really changed, the clock still ticked the same.

The radio in her ear changed to Top Forty Country, and Beth had a little anxiety attack and hung up. She would make another cup of coffee and try again later, after she had rehearsed just what she would say.

Beth had known Billy Ray Warren ever since junior high, but had trusted him—really found that he was a man she could trust—for the past eighteen years. It was an involved story, the way she and Billy Ray had connected, one that she wasn't particularly proud of, one she had never shared with anyone, especially not with Perry.

Years ago, before Perry went off to the Marines, he enrolled out at Shawnee County Junior College, the local two-year college, set to play fullback for a couple of years, even though everybody told him he should have gone straight over to East Texas State, that he was good enough to play there. But things didn't work out at SCJC, and before the end of the first season, Perry had a falling out with the head football coach. The coach had recruited a black kid from Houston with an SAT score in double digits who would play there, as it turned out, only long enough to get his grade point average up so he could transfer down to Texas A&M. The transfer was a done deal, everybody knew, and the kid was good, faster than Perry, with moves, a stutterstep and go, a hit-the-line-and-spin technique that no one around there had seen before.

Perry was relegated to second string and before the season was over had quit the team and signed up for his three years in the Marines. He vowed to come back and play, but he would be bigger and tougher and stronger. But that sixty-pound pack had ruined his knees, and then there was the unfortunate encounter with Mouth in the Philippines. Perry limped back home and sneaked off to East Texas State where in three-and-a-half years he got his teaching degree.

The fall he had played football at SCJC, Perry started dating Beth, who was a senior at Brown Valley, a little town twenty miles to the east of Cottonwood, where her daddy was a pharmacist at the only drugstore around.

By Christmas of that year Beth considered them engaged.

They slipped off to Shreveport one contrived weekend and spent part of a night in the darkness of a lights-out, blinds-drawn room in the Sands Motel out on the road to Bossier City, Beth never unhooking her bra, her panties still looped around one of her legs. Except for Perry grunting and pushing between her legs in the dark, it hardly even qualified as grown-up sex.

Beth was pretty then, she knew, her face light and full of hope in the high school yearbook, and she felt betrayed when Perry dropped out of college and started his three-year Marine hitch, although he made all sorts of promises, which, she had to admit even now, he had kept.

But for the first months he was gone, Beth felt as if she had been tricked. Having sex before you were married might not be a big deal to girls in Dallas or wherever, but for Beth, from a conservative Methodist family in Brown Valley, it was momentous.

Beth finished out high school in a daze, writing Perry almost everyday, the letters she now could see, silly and girlish and oh, so needy. Perry wrote back that he had made Lance Corporal right away and had a marksmanship medal. Then his letters came infrequently and when he shipped out to the Pacific, they stopped almost altogether.

Beth enrolled in SCJC, majoring in elementary ed, and in a basic psychology course found herself next to Billy Ray Warren.

Beth dialed the number again, and again the woman put her on hold, her voice a little waspish this time.

The rest Beth could hardly bear to think about now, betrayal not something to file away in your favorite memories box, although the memory of being desired and pursued and finally being seduced—that was indeed the correct word—for Billy Ray Warren, with his outlandishly lanky frame and his western boots and his Adam's apple that bobbed too noticeably when he talked, had courted and seduced Beth, all with hat in hand, in a gentlemanly sort of way. Until that afternoon in the ample front seat of Billy Ray's pickup when he told her in no uncertain terms what he wanted, and Beth had in some mood of defiance to Perry opened herself up to him.

She had touched him "down there," as she later thought about it, had seen his hard smoothness that afternoon parked in the woods near Clear Creek, this incident of sexual openness occurring before she actually had seen or touched Perry. She got some perverse enjoyment from knowing that, the touching and the seeing held on to over all these years as the one thing she had of her own, something that all of Perry's ramming and grunting and humping could never take away, and often while she lay under her husband taking his sweaty thickness with her eyes wide open and a smile on her face, she could imagine once again Billy Ray's silky leanness.

When Perry had left for the Marines Beth felt like she was a notch in his M-1, but with Billy Ray she knew she had been special.

"He'll be right with you," the woman now said, breaking Beth's reverie. "Can I say who's calling?"

"No," Beth said, feeling her breath catch. Then quietly, in almost a whisper, she said, "It's Beth Reynolds."

In a minute Billy Ray came on the line, all business. "Yes, Beth. How can I help you?" Polite as always, maybe a trace of affection in his voice, but never an intonation to betray their past intimacy. A rare man, Beth figured, not to hold that over her in some way, if only to build his ego from time to time.

Beth could picture him now, stretched way back in his swivel chair, boots crossed on the glass-topped desk, eyeing the five-by-seven gold-framed studio picture of Sue Ellen and their three kids on the wall in front of him. She could imagine the bump in his jeans. Beth smiled, then got serious.

"Can we talk? I mean on the phone? It's about Perry." She took a shallow breath. "I'm worried." Beth heard Billy Ray shift around, the chair squeak and roll, and she could imagine him now leaning forward, intent on her words, maybe even seeing quickly into the future, that Perry would be out of the picture and he could, now that he was worn out with Sue Ellen and those three kids, run off with Beth, his one and only ever true love.

Then when Beth began to cry, he said he would be right out, but she said no, she had to go to work, that she was okay, and it all poured out, Perry's late nights (no, she knew it wasn't another woman), and the odd phone calls, and hauling his boat off at all hours of the night.

"Is there anything else?"

And Beth remembered the books and magazines—The Hunter's Bible, Soldier of Fortune and Survival, and on and on, hidden in the bottom of a box in his closet, under his duck-hunting camouflage slicker. The way a more normally obsessed man might have a stack of Playboys or Penthouses secreted away.

"Let me bird dog a few leads," Billy Ray said. Beth could hear him slide his wad of tobacco from one cheek to the other. "Make a couple of phone calls. I'll let you know what I find out. In the meantime keep your eyes open."

"Billy Ray," Beth said, and waited a moment. "I'm not trying to ruin my life," she said, "just trying to save it."

"It's between the two of us. I'll keep it quiet." Then he

hesitated, took his moment of silence. "Same as always," he said, quietly, and hung up.

Wednesday morning Beth had just gotten out of the shower and gone to the kitchen where she rinsed a half pound of pinto beans and put them on to soak. The phone rang and she started to let her machine answer, afraid it might be Edwina needing her to go to Piggly Wiggly that afternoon or have her pick up a prescription. But she answered it anyway.

"Mrs. Reynolds?" a man's voice asked. "This is Gerald Kemp, with the Dallas office of the Bureau of Alcohol, Tobacco and Firearms." Then he stopped a minute, and Beth could hear some papers shuffling. "A Deputy Sheriff William Warren, Shawnee County, called our office on Monday. He relayed to me that you have some concerns about your husband, a Perry Dale Reynolds. Is that right?"

"Well, yes, I suppose I did," Beth said, and suddenly she felt betrayed by Billy Ray, the first time ever, although what else she had expected to come of her call to him she didn't know. Betrayed by Billy Ray, and overcome by a sad and desperate sense of loyalty to Perry, who had, after all slept beside her—hostile, acrimonious, bitter, and resentful much of the time—but beside her, and that had to count for something, didn't it? If POWs develop a bond with their captors after years of confinement, why shouldn't she feel faithful to the man who was her husband and the father of her daughter? A pointed sense of loyalty overwhelmed her.

The ATF man, this strange Mr. Kemp from Dallas, kept going on about how he and Beth, "perhaps with Deputy Sheriff Warren might want to get together" to pursue this and that, and Beth wanted to say that it was all a mistake, a joke, that Billy Ray—not William at all—was an old friend and this was only a way to, to . . . what?

"Maybe we'd do well to meet, at your convenience, of course, and discuss this further."

And just as suddenly as they had combined to take her over, the loyalty, the faithfulness, and the defensiveness that Beth had conjured up wafted away, and she knew in her heart, deep inside of the Beth who had never really loved Perry or liked Perry or respected Perry but had lived a horrible sin–against-God mistake for this far into her life, had to meet, must meet with this strange man in order to save what spark there still might be, not of her marriage, but of her spirit and of her soul.

SEVEN

LIQUOR STORES in Texas open at 10:00 in the
morning and lock their doors at 9:00 at night,
Mondays through Saturdays. They are closed, by
God, and by the state legislature on Sundays. There is no
arguing with the hours, no cheating. You break the rules and
the Texas Alcohol Beverage Commission boys will be on
your ass, padlock your front door.

Reynolds had maneuvered his way through the eighties,
the dogpaddling head of a Texas bank until he got arm-
weary and sank. If he had learned nothing else, it was keep
your operation clean—at least on the surface, where it
counts. Whether it was a gaggle of bank auditors or a bunch
of beer cops from the TABC, it didn't matter. Then and now.
Only the faces change. Reynolds didn't live in fear—that
word was too strong—but the bank shutdown had left him
with a residue of dread in his gut that made him cautious.

To be safe Reynolds kept "bar time" on his clock behind
the counter, set fifteen minutes fast so he could herd the
hangers-on out early into the Texas nights. And he didn't

mind kicking butt. No minors, no queer IDs. Reynolds took no shit, no wise-ass stories from teenagers. He'd been one himself.

Before he opened at 10:00 Reynolds kept the front blinds down, the "NOPE" sign up so he could have the place to himself. Now, this Saturday morning, in the middle of December, Reynolds checked the clock—a quarter to 10:00, liquor store time. The sun rose low in the southeast in the winter and now slits of bright rays lined the wooden floor and shimmered across the rows of bottles.

Reynolds opened a new CD, one that UPS Carl had dropped off on Friday while he was gone. The CD had been on the counter this morning when Reynolds slipped in the back door with his third mug of coffee, licking powdered sugar off of his fingers. The package had been opened, but the CD still was shrink-wrapped. Reynolds gave a little laugh. Joy couldn't help herself—she always opened all of his mail, always grabbed the telephone before Reynolds could make a move.

At first Reynolds thought she was possessive or jealous or something, but after he got to know Joy he understood that she simply couldn't stand to be left out of anything.

Anything, in this case, being Beethoven's complete piano sonatas. Reynolds smiled, wishing he could have seen Joy's reaction when she tore into the package.

Reynolds popped the cassette in for a quick listen. For a couple of minutes he stood there, his eyes closed, one hand on the counter for balance. He started to move a little, felt the tingling need to glide around the store, but he wore his flip-flops this morning and no socks, and he still felt a little rumble inside from those early morning donuts.

Besides, he wasn't sure about these sonatas. They were pretty dense going and seemed to lack the same energy as the Goldberg Variations. Technically challenging—even Reynolds could appreciate that—but the music seemed to short out somewhere between his brain and his gut.

Maybe he had bought the tape for the wrong reason—the old "should" problem that always led him down the wrong cow trail. Did he order Beethoven's sonatas because he wanted to hear them, or because he felt he should want to hear them? Or maybe he did it to piss Joy off. Or maybe to claim a little territory, for his own self, whatever in the hell that was, by latching on to something that would keep everyone else away. Beethoven as a psychological weapon.

The third sonata began, upbeat, dense, packed with notes, more notes than he could imagine, and he tried to see the score in his mind, but it came up crowded and busy as a bucket of minnows.

The tape whirred on. Not bad, he thought. Not Bach, however. Bach delivered that irresistible urge to spin and dance around the room. Might not be all Beethoven's fault, he admitted. Maybe sober mornings had something to do with it. He'd have to try it after 9:00 one night, when he closed the store down and sipped on some Old Fitz while he waited for Joy.

The back door popped open. It was Joy, her ponytail dangled heavy, still damp from the shower. Her Next to Nowhere uniform hung on her, seemed a couple of sizes too big; it camouflaged her breasts, straightened out the nice roundness of her ass. She looked ordinary to Reynolds this morning, older than twenty-six, for sure, and Reynolds felt sadness and regret flow over him. For Joy or for him he didn't know. But it was as if some heaviness had come into the room and would squash them both.

"Here's a sandwich," she said. "Ham and cheese. For later."

She sat the napkin-wrapped sandwich on top of a slide-top cooler. "I made one for Deanie, too."

Reynolds nodded. "This won't work," he said. "I already screwed up having my own kids. I'm just not the daddy type. This isn't fair. Not for Deanie, not for you. And damn sure not for me."

Joy started to flare up, but Reynolds cut her off, put his hand in the air, the universal "Whoa" sign. "It's okay for today, maybe for a few more days. But Joy, you know me. I'm just not cut out for this family shit."

"It is only for a few more days. Until Deanie gets Christmas break. Then her daddy will take her for two weeks and after that, well, I'll work something out. I've told you that and told you that."

"Hell, I heard you, and I heard you." Reynolds glanced at the clock: ten-fifteen. He heard somebody rattling the front door. "Shit, I've gotta open up."

"Reynolds," Joy said, "don't give me a hard time about this. It's out of my control. And Deanie's no trouble at all. She'll sleep late as usual and then eat some donuts and watch TV. Her sandwich is in the refrigerator. She won't bother you. I promise. And I'll try to get off early tonight. But if I don't work, I don't get paid. And if I don't get paid Deanie and I, well, I don't know exactly what we could do. Bo Reed's bad sick, for God's sake. And Mama's worn out from that piss-ant job. She won't be able to watch out for Deanie again for who knows how long. I didn't plan this, you know."

She turned to leave. Joy looked a lot more alive now, a lot prettier, too, Reynolds had to admit. It was as if he had splashed a bucket of starter fluid on her fire. And somehow Reynolds now felt himself fill up with the possibilities of his life. He raised his hand again, two fingers spread in the universal peace sign. They would fight later. "Adios, darlin'. Don't worry about me and Deanie. We'll be good injuns. For today. Bring home a sackful of tips." Reynolds started towards the front, then stopped. "You got time for a quickie?" he asked, a big grin on his face.

"You're a bastard, Reynolds. A real bastard. A quickie nine years ago started all the troubles of my life. Now if I thought another quickie would fix things I'd be out of my panties in a second. But I don't think so." Joy shook her head. "I'm sorry this is all so hard," she said, softening a little bit.

Then she turned to go but caught herself. "Do me a favor, will you Reynolds. If Deanie does come over turn that damned music off, will you. I want her to grow up a normal kid. Okay?"

Reynolds grinned, turned the volume up a little, and Joy was gone. The door banged behind her.

By 11:00 things got quiet; December was a rough month out around the lake, too cold to fish, too cold for beer. Right before Christmas Reynolds would move some fancy packaged whiskey and tequila, but most of the serious drinkers stocked up in the superstores around Dallas. The big boys could sell it cheaper than Reynolds could buy it.

Reynolds accepted that—it was the way America worked. Reynolds sold booze of convenience.

After the sun got high Reynolds pulled the blinds all the way up and began clearing out the windows so that he could squeegee them clean. Appearances were important, he knew, not to Stick or the other regulars, maybe, but a Dallas woman might wander by in her blue-jean skirt and red boots and frilly blouse, maybe one driving a Land Rover or a Jeep Wagoneer, a woman with a hundred-dollar haircut and with class, maybe divorced or scouting around, maybe Reynolds' ticket out of here. You never could tell who might cross the threshold of Lake City Liquors. Reynolds was no damned Boy Scout, but he damned sure would be prepared.

Reynolds wore his khakis on Saturdays, and a soft, blue cotton button-down-collar shirt. He slid his flip-flops under the counter, slipped on some loafers without socks. He knew what women wanted, someone dancing that line between safety and risk. Controlled risk, but big enough for a woman to live within. Risky enough to enlarge her life.

He'd made his mistakes before, with Sheila, but he was a goddamn banker then, out of character completely, and Sheila got bored. Just as well. Reynolds was different now, had begun to find himself. He checked his reflection in the window. Not bad. Mornings were better than nights. At night the neon beer signs created a problem, sort of washed him out, turned him some off-shade of blue.

After noon Deanie popped in the back door full of questions, full of complaints: "When will Mama be back? Cartoons are over. TV is boring. Can I have a Big Red?"

Reynolds stopped her before she got to her disaster questions: "What would we do if a tornado hit? What would you do if a robber came in and he had a gun? What would happen if the lake flooded and the bridge washed away and we were trapped?" Disaster questions were Deanie's specialty, and they drove Reynolds nuts.

Real quick Reynolds put her to work, gave her a pad and a ballpoint pen and set her up in the back room counting beer. "This is called taking inventory, Deanie. I do it once every month, and I'll pay you Deanie, if you do this right. No money, but anything on the rack you want—peanuts, M&M's, beef jerky sticks, sunflower seeds."

"There's too many," Deanie complained, taking in the

stacked cases of beer. But she liked this, Reynolds could tell, playing grown-up in a liquor store. See, he thought, it starts early, wanting to walk on the edge of risk. Hanging around a store full of booze at eight years old provided a decent amount of excitement he would guess. The allure of the forbidden. Well, time would take care of that soon enough, he knew.

Reynolds kept the back room orderly enough, if the delivery men didn't screw it up. So he started out the inventory list for her, Bud and Miller, regular and light, Lone Star and Busch and Old Milwaukee, Pearl and Pabst, Corona and Coors. "You find some more kinds, just add them to the bottom. Okay?"

Deanie nodded. She was quick and bright, cute, but a real pain-in-the-ass in progress. Deanie would turn out a lot like Joy, Reynolds figured, with those washed out green eyes, her long skinny legs, her full lips.

Reynolds checked on her from time to time. Deanie stayed hard after it. Work never hurt anybody, he thought. He wished Larry and Garry were around more, but they had been around, with him and Sheila, when the boys were Deanie's age, on up until they were eleven or twelve, and Reynolds had never involved them in work. He had left all the kid raising to Sheila. But what could a kid do in a bank, anyway? And he wouldn't want a kid of his helping out here, hanging around a liquor store. Not the kind of place kids should be. Deanie was different, he thought, but couldn't come up with why. Except that she belonged to Joy and not to him.

In the afternoon things got quiet and Reynolds slipped over to the trailer to wash up, check the refrigerator for something sweet, maybe some Blue Bell ice cream. He couldn't have been gone more than five minutes, probably three or four, he would swear, but when he got back some fellow was at the counter talking to Deanie, who had come out from the back.

Reynolds glanced out the front window, wondering how he hadn't heard the man drive up, and then he spotted his car parked off to one side, a soft green Ford sedan with black sidewall tires and a miniature antenna curling up from the back fender. Shit and god almighty, Reynolds thought, he's a damned beer cop. Working undercover. Caught an eight-year-old girl minding the store. Well, this makes my god-damned day.

The man nodded when Reynolds came in. He wore sun-shades and a short brim, western-style hat, navy blue slacks and a white shirt and tie. Round-toed boots gleamed. His windbreaker was zipped up halfway.

"Nice help you've got here," the man said, nodding at Deanie.

"Can I help you?" Reynolds asked. He motioned for Deanie to leave, but she stood there holding her inventory.

"There's more Bud than I have room for," she said, holding up the inventory for Reynolds to see.

The fellow laughed, moved over to the window that opened up over the lake and the boat ramp below. "Nice view from here. The boat ramp yours?"

Reynolds nodded. "Deanie," he said, "that's enough for now. Come here, pick out some candy, whatever you want, and try the TV again. I'll check on you in a little bit."

"I need to finish first. The Coors is in the back, but it's stacked too high for me to count."

"Okay, okay. We'll do it later. Now go on."

"Can I have peanuts and candy and a Big Red?"

"Take it and go. Whatever you want." Reynolds shook his head and tried to grin but couldn't.

Deanie grabbed a handful of packages from the rack, reached deep in the cooler for her drink and raced out the back door.

"Damned kids," Reynolds muttered, and the fellow laughed.

"Your granddaughter?" he asked.

Shit, Reynolds thought, if you weren't a beer boy I'd kick your ass out of here. "Not exactly," he said.

The man turned back to the window while he talked. "You charge to use the ramp, I guess."

"Nope. It's free. A service to the public from Lake City Liquors. Just what the sign down there says. I try to treat folks right. Yeah, fair and square. That's the only way to go."

The man studied the lake a minute more. Reynolds began to get antsy. He glanced at his liquor license on the wall to make sure it hadn't expired.

"I'll bet from here you can see damn near everything going on." He pointed towards the lake. "You know. Down there."

"If I stood here all day I guess I could. But not after dark, not when I'm closed." Reynolds grabbed the broom and began to sweep in a little circle. Then he stopped, holding the broom in front of him, gesturing with it while he talked. "You know, I work for a living, mind my own business up here. As long as folks don't trash it out down there I could care less what they do."

The man whirled around. "No need to get hot," he said, "I'm just doing my job, too."

"Hey," Reynolds said, "I'll keep the kid out of here. She's not really working, you know, just bored, and her mama's working. The first time she's ever done this." Reynolds gave a nervous laugh. "No harm, no foul, they say. Live and let live. C'est la vie."

The man pulled his sunglasses off, pointed them at Reynolds, all of a sudden impatient. "I don't give a damn about that kid," he said. "You can put the whole kindergarten on the payroll for all I care."

And all at once Reynolds knew he had this figured wrong. This was no state beer boy.

The stranger stepped closer to Reynolds and handed him a card he held between two stubby fingers.

Gerald Kemp
Investigator
Alcohol, Tobacco and Firearms.

"I guess you know a Perry Dale Reynolds," he said referring to a little spiral top notebook.

"Perry?" Reynolds said. He was puzzled. "Perry's my brother, but hell, he doesn't even drink."

"You see him often? He come out here? You let him use your boat ramp?"

"Well, hell mister," Reynolds said, "if this has to do with what happened in the Marines, well, I just found out about that the other day, and it surprised the hell out of me. I mean, like I say, Perry doesn't drink, is a three-time-a-week Christian, and teaches school. Hey, he's straight arrow."

"Does he stop by here?"

"Never put foot inside that door," Reynolds said. "You must not know much about brothers. Perry would carry his boat six miles on his back not to be seen around here, around his brother's liquor store."

Kemp kept quiet, pacing back and forth slowly in front of the window.

"If you don't mind my asking," Reynolds finally said, "what's your big concern with Perry?"

Just then Stick came busting through the door, his coveralls zipped up to his neck, his hands and arms smeared with grease. "Man it's colder than a well digger's. . . ." He cut it off when he spotted Reynolds' chalky face, the dressed-up fellow next to him. "Colder than a well digger's shovel," he finished.

Reynolds nodded. Stick was nobody's fool. He put his head down and made a straight line to the beer cooler.

Gerald Kemp eased over to the window once more, checked the lake, the bridge leading from across the way. "I'll be stopping by again, Mr. Reynolds. I'd buy a six pack, but I've got some work to do." At the door he stopped, watched Stick for a moment, then spoke quietly, low, so that Stick wouldn't hear. "A nice clean place here. I'll bet you run a good store. Be a shame to screw up and lose it. Wouldn't it?"

"I don't know what in the hell you're after," Reynolds said.

"You've got my card. A phone call now is a lot cleaner than a subpoena later. You'll be doing everyone a favor— even your brother—in the long run." He turned, and in a moment was gone. Reynolds watched the Ford kick up gravel in the parking lot as Kemp hurried off.

"What the shit," Reynolds yelled. He pulled back the broom and threw it, the wooden handle clattering across the floor until it banged to a stop against the closed front door.

EIGHT

NO BEETHOVEN tonight. No Bach. No dancing and sliding around that slick wooden floor in his socks and jockey shorts. There would be no Garth Brooks later. Reynolds sat in the Saturday night dark of the liquor store and waited for Joy, the "NOPE" sign turned out to face the parking lot. He waited behind the counter in a swivel chair he had managed to salvage when the bank shut down, his bare feet propped on a four-case-high stack of Lone Star, the boom box, the bottle of Old Fitz 1849, the beer cooler to one side, all in easy reach.

This was a pissed-off, *Blue Eyes Crying in the Rain,* Lone Star-guzzling, straight-from-the-bottle whiskey sort of night.

Joy had told him she'd be back early if she could. Well, for some damned reason she couldn't, and she hadn't, and her reason had better be good, and if not good, at least original. Reynolds had had it with women and their made-up stories. He was in a take-no-crap sort of mood.

Women. Shit. Even girls. Even Deanie. Deanie was a nice enough kid, but she almost got his ass burned today. If Gerald

Kemp had been a beer cop, Reynolds could have had a thirty-day vacation. Joy had no right to leave Deanie here with him. This wasn't a marriage, for God's sake, it was a coupling of convenience. No more. No less.

The last time Reynolds checked on Deanie she was sprawled across his bed in the trailer fascinated by some TV special on avalanches, shrieking when tons of snow rumbled down picturesque peaks and wiped out a line of Swiss chalets. Reynolds had brought her some cheese and peanut butter crackers from the store, and a quart of Bloody Mary mix.

Deanie didn't even look up from the TV, but as he was leaving, she said, "Reynolds, what if it snowed, real hard, and we were trapped here in the trailer, and Mama was at work. What would we do?"

"This is Texas, Deanie. Snow today, gone tomorrow."

"Oh, Reynolds," she said. "I mean really."

"That's really, Deanie. Now turn off the tube and go to sleep. It's late." On the TV a couple of skiers raced down a slope, just ahead of a giant snow slide that quickly overtook them. Deanie shrieked again, and Reynolds shook his head and left.

Reynolds stopped between the trailer and the store and pissed, aiming his stream out to one side, weaving a little as he took in the enormity of the sky. The clouds had blown to the southeast now and the north wind whipped around the trailer. "Son of a bitch," Reynolds said, zipping up. "Freeze my ass out here," and he wished he'd grabbed his jacket, but didn't want to face another disaster question from Deanie.

Back in the liquor store he lit the big space heater and for a minute stood with his back to it, warming his hands behind him. From there he could see the lake, rippled black velvet.

Why the hell would Perry be messing around down there? He came up blank.

He moved to the counter, counted the seven empty long-necks lined up there. He popped Willie out, Leonard Cohen in. God, he thought, this will do it. Want to get down inside yourself, wallow in the shit of your life? Try Leonard Cohen, his whiskey voice and easy poetry. This was hide-your-guns, flush-your-drugs, call-the-suicide-hotline kind of music. On nights like this when he found himself trapped in a slough of self-pity, Reynolds loved it.

He had almost called Perry but waited too late. By the time the Lone Star and the Old Fitz gave him courage, he no longer trusted his brain or his mouth. He decided to wait. Think this through. In all likelihood there had been a mistake. Just check their history, the ATF boys were bad about mistakes.

Something minor might be going on; Ray Senior had indicated there was more when he and Reynolds had their talk on the ride out to the lake. But the feds could get all constipated over nothing. Maybe Reynolds would borrow a typewriter and send Perry an anonymous warning note. A "You'd better stop whatever it is you're doing," note. But that seemed awfully vague.

Reynolds took another sip from the whiskey bottle. He laughed. Maybe when Perry got his warning note, he would give up church, or give up sex—if he and Beth hadn't given up on sex long ago. Reynolds couldn't imagine Beth being sexy, not with Perry. Or maybe she was okay—Reynolds had a time or two imagined the possibilities, noted her potential. Maybe living with Perry was her problem. He was too careful.

And dull, dull, dull.

Well, Reynolds might have it bad, but he wasn't dull, and neither were his women.

For a couple of seconds the flash of a single headlight illuminated the store, and now Joy's car rattled in beside the trailer. Reynolds heard the car door slam, and in a moment heard the trailer door click open and Joy fussing at Deanie in a loud whisper, before that door slammed, too.

Reynolds straightened up the store while Joy showered. He tossed the sack of empties in the recycle bin, then toted them out back, and dumped them in with the rest of the trash.

What the hell. He was sick of doing the right thing, being bullied by everyone. "Shit on you all," he said out loud. He wished Sheila was here. He'd tell her off, and Perry, he'd tell him to stop being a let's-pretend do-gooder and straighten up his ass. Edwina could just shut that bible crap up and leave him alone, and Joy—well, Joy was fixing to get hers.

The back door burst open. "God, what a day," Joy said. "God, what a night. I need a drink."

"On the counter," Reynolds said.

Joy took the bottle, looked around. "You have a glass?"

"Under the counter."

"And ice, I guess, is in the freezer. Right?"

"Right on, sister."

Leonard Cohen was going on about Joan of Arc, now, the lyrics too symbolic for Reynolds tonight. Fire and wood and flames. Love and suffering and death. All too confusing, not enough to the point. Reynolds popped Leonard out, Willie back in. "Fucking 'Stardust,'" he muttered. "Shit." He popped Willie out, popped Hank Williams in. Beer-drinking music for sure.

"Are you okay?" Joy held her drink, stirred the bourbon

and water with her pinky. She seemed uneasy, a little too loud with her talk, like she was afraid of short stretches of silence, like the best defense is a good you-know-what.

"What happened to Garth Brooks?" she asked.

"Beer boys scared his ass off," Reynolds said. He took his feet down and without looking reached behind him for another Lone Star.

"Well, my day was hell," Joy said. "Since you asked."

"Cut the fucking sarcasm, Joy," Reynolds said. "Tell me now. Just why your day was hell." He twisted the top on the beer, let the foam bubble up, run down the sides of the bottle.

Joy told him, her voice quick and tight, how Doris, the other waitress, had called in sick so she had to work late, and how the bus boy tore up his leg when he slid his motorcycle under a parked semi, and on and on. All of a sudden Reynolds understood where Deanie got her infatuation with disasters, how a disaster might just put the grand explanation on damned near everything.

Joy moved around, restless while she talked. Reminded Reynolds of something he'd seen, something he'd heard before, but he couldn't quite place it. Reynolds gave Joy a C- for originality, a C+ for sincerity. Borderline passing.

Reynolds shook his head. "Life's a bitch," he said. Then he straightened up in his chair, sat his beer down hard on the counter. "Deanie can't stay. She's got to go."

Joy started to fire up, but Reynolds cut her off, told her about Deanie coming over to the store—when she wasn't supposed to, when Joy had told him she wouldn't—and how Reynolds put her to work, "To teach her some values," Reynolds said.

"From you?" Joy said. "That'll ruin her for sure."

Then Reynolds told her about the scare with the ATF

man, the way Reynolds thought he was a beer boy and would close the place down with Deanie there working. But Reynolds didn't mention Perry. He needed to get that straight in his head before he took that any further.

"What did he want?" Joy asked, "The ATF fellow."

"Wondered if I had seen any suspicious activity around here. Especially down around the boat ramp."

"Well, I'll sure keep my eyes open," Joy said, getting all bright-eyed. "And don't you worry, not even one minute. I'll see that Deanie doesn't ever put her foot in here again. I promise."

Joy moved over close to Reynolds and gave him a little pat on the arm, but looked beyond him, as if she saw some place in the distance and Reynolds wasn't—and never would be—there.

And then it came to Reynolds, all this nicer-than-it-needs-to-be talk, all the conciliatory, out-of-character bowing and scraping. Yeah, he remembered, he knew where that kind of talk came from.

It must have been ten years ago by now. Or more. He and Sheila had gone out to the little country club for a Fourth of July pro-am tournament. Not a big deal, but Sheila had taken up golf a few months before, so she drove out early, got her a cart and followed the action around the course. Cottonwood Country Club doesn't even have eighteen holes, you just play the regular tees for the front nine, then tee off twenty yards closer on each hole for the back nine. Thirty-seven par on the front nine, thirty-five for the balance. A nice, neat, boring seventy-two.

Reynolds came out later, lounged around the pool sipping a couple of drinks, bikini watching, waiting for the barbecue to finish smoking for the night's big dinner and dance. Well, the brisket and ribs came and went, the band fiddled and picked, Reynolds played a little five-card stud in the game room, lost fifty bucks. About 10:30 he went home. Ten years ago the boys were still little, so Reynolds chewed a couple of mints, drove the babysitter back to her house, and called it a night. But somehow he couldn't sleep. He clicked on the TV, watched a couple of rounds of a Muhammad Ali / Sonny Liston "Great Fights of the Century" re-run. But all that dancing and jabbing and feinting and slugging agitated him. He clicked that off, got a bowl of chocolate fudge nut ice cream and sat in the dark, waiting—for what he didn't exactly know.

Sheila came in about midnight, slipping through the house all quiet until she saw Reynolds still awake, then she got blustery for a minute, said how she tried to find him at the country club, that was why she was so late. And then, you wouldn't believe it, but her Land Rover had a flat, and her friend Jeanie had to drive her into town, but they stopped at the Pitt Grill for coffee. Nervous talk. The truth is never nervous—that Reynolds knew.

"That's how you got grass stains on your pants?" he asked. "Sitting on the goddamn red vinyl booth at the fucking Pitt Grill?" Reynolds gave her a D for originality, a D- for sincerity.

Sheila brushed at her pants, tossed her frosted hair. "Oh, what the hell," she said, and came clean, so to speak. A third-rate pro-golfer, trying to pick up an easy trophy and a little expense money at a hoe-daddy tournament, instead picked up an easy lay on the smooth Tiff grass of the seventh green.

Tonight, here in the dark of the liquor store, was re-run time, only it wasn't Sheila this round, it was Joy. Joy illuminated by the flames from the gas heater, the soft blue glow of a Coors waterfall in the window, Reynolds listening while Joy danced her words around in that same quick way. Joy's story wasn't a flat on her one-eyed car and coffee at the Pitt Grill, but Doris, the sick waitress, and the bad luck busboy. But it was the same nervous talk, filling in all the blank spaces to keep the truth from seeping in.

Reynolds didn't hang around for more, didn't have the heart to press the real story out of Joy, wouldn't turn on the liquor store lights, didn't want to see this version of the grass stains. Joy had left him, and Reynolds knew it. Not physically, but she had left. That string that had held them together for almost six months had snapped.

Reynolds felt too old, too worn down by everything for a big fight so he told Joy she could stay in his trailer behind the liquor store for a couple of weeks more, while she found another place for her and Deanie.

Joy cried. He had never seen her cry, and it wasn't for losing him, Reynolds knew. But he was tired of being an asshole, and Joy didn't have much choice, nowhere else to go at the time, and Reynolds had an out, he could stay in town at his mama's house, the house he grew up in.

Ray Senior was still hiding out at his place up on the lake, and the second bedroom there was the same, hadn't changed since he and then Perry had left home all those years before.

Joy stayed in the store, sipped on her drink, while Reynolds grabbed some clothes and took off. By the time he got to town he felt agitated, as if he had impulsively made a wrong decision that he would regret.

He stopped in the Midnight Express bar, a private, members-and-motel-guests-only sort of place hidden in the dark recesses of the Holiday Star Motel. The bar was almost empty. He got a draft beer and moved to a booth in the corner. He put the glass on the table but didn't sit down. In a minute he went to the pay phone. He'd bounce this whole thing off of Sheila. And maybe some strange, lonely woman would waltz in while he was on the phone.

Reynolds filled Sheila in, making Joy out to be more pathetic than she was, making himself more gallant. "Joy's not much more than a kid," Reynolds said, explaining everything. "And she's broke." It was nearly midnight now, and he hated it, but more than a few years divorced and Reynolds still had the urge to call Sheila on nights like this, when he got lonely or needed to work out a problem. "It's no big deal. I can stay here in town, at Mama's for a few nights, and drive back and forth out to the lake. I couldn't just kick Joy out."

"You're such a softie," Sheila said, "and getting old, too. Listen, it's late. I'm busy now," she said. "I'll call you in a day or two. But let me give you some advice. Stay away from those cute young things, Reynolds. They'll break your heart. Take your money, too. If you had any, that is."

Reynolds heard a laugh in the background, a man's laugh, and he remembered why he and Sheila had split. "You bitch," Reynolds muttered.

Sheila laughed. "Poor Reynolds, drunk again and all alone."

Reynolds heard the man laugh once more, this time louder, as if he had leaned close to the phone to listen. Reynolds hung up.

He paid up and left. Outside in the parking lot the cold surprised him. A fine mist hung in the air and a thin glaze of ice clattered to the asphalt when he slammed his car door. He drove cautiously, squinting through the scrape and drag of windshield wipers for icy spots on the road, watching for the town's lone deputy who patrolled the streets at night.

Reynolds parked out in front of his mother's house, at an odd angle he noticed the next day, and pissed in the barren flowerbed next to the front porch. He slipped in quietly, a little drunk, maybe more than a little. He shook his head, swore off booze, swore off Joy, swore off Sheila, swore off all the women in the world.

In Edwina's front room he brushed against a scraggly cedar tree adorned with ornaments and smothered with tinsel and fake icicles. As he passed, a glass globe hit the linoleum floor with a crack. "Shit," he whispered. He bent over to pick up the pieces and felt a wad of icicles cling to his head. He straightened up and with his foot pushed the broken glass back under the tree. He waited a minute in the dark, surprised his mama hadn't waddled out to check on the noise. I'll get up early, he thought, pulling the icicles out of his hair, and clean this mess up before Mama finds it.

But he knew he wouldn't, and he didn't really care. A broken Christmas ball and a few icicles on the floor might just distract his mama from the bigger things—how Reynolds was "living in sin with that Joy girl" and how Sheila was "really a good woman who would come back if only Reynolds would ask her."

Reynolds moaned out loud. You dumb bastard, he thought, and if he hadn't chased that last bourbon with a beer he would have crept back out and retreated to the lake to reclaim his own place like a man. As shitty as it might be, it was his. But the night was gone, and Reynolds was too, he knew—a little unsteady to drive back out to the lake and deal with Joy again. Too late for all of that.

His bedroom, the one he shared with Perry all those years, was down the hall to the right, and as Reynolds tiptoed on through the little house, he noticed the glow from the kitchen light. Maybe mama left a piece of her buttermilk pie out on the counter, he thought, but shook his head. That, along with the broken ornament, would have to wait until morning.

The bedroom looked the same. Model airplanes, the old paper-glued-over-balsa-wood kind, still circled over his bed, and Perry's old high school letter jacket hung limp and moth-tattered on the back of a chair. On the desk a stack of 1960s U. S. News and World Reports still warned of the dangers of communism. A New Testament—one his mama had put there—now held the magazines in place.

Damn but the room was cold. He stretched out on the narrow bed and kicked off his shoes. There was a space heater against the wall, but Reynolds didn't want to asphyxiate himself. Not yet, he thought, but couldn't help thinking how much easier that would be for them all. A relief to Sheila, and to his mama and to Joy. Perry, too. The twins, Larry and Garry, might be sad a few weeks, but they hardly knew him now. Maybe that was just as well. Only his daddy might really care, and Ray Senior had hid out so deep in the woods, word might not get to him for days.

"Uh uh," Reynolds said. "Not yet. I still have a few things to do." But what those things might be seemed awfully trivial tonight, floating drunkenly around the little room.

Still might be a good woman out there somewhere, he figured, one who would treat him right. Now that would be worth hanging around for. And he wouldn't want to die broke, that's not what he had planned on at all, and given a few more years and a little luck he would turn the damned money thing around.

Then there were Larry and Garry. If Sheila would only get her claws out, stop poisoning Reynolds every time she opened her mouth, they might come around more often, maybe even move back after they finished school. Would he want that? Or did he think he should want that? Teenaged boys, with their hormones going bonkers and their need for cars and money, and maybe even college—Reynolds wasn't ready for all of that. Maybe they were better off with Sheila, where her daddy could spoil them all. All those vague long-ings and scattered thoughts spun around the room as he sat back up on the edge of the bed and wrestled out of his clothes. Finally down to his jockey shorts, he slid down under a Star of Texas quilt. His breath made soft clouds that floated off into the room. Then everything twirled for a few moments and Reynolds was gone.

NINE

DOTTIE HAIRSTON, from next door, out searching for her cat the next morning, spotted Edwina crumpled at the bottom of the icy back steps. Edwina's hip had snapped in two places, and her hand, even in death, still gripped a dishtowel. "Lord help us, Lord help us," was all Dottie could say as she bent down to check Edwina's stiff body.

Dottie knew Reynolds was there. She had spotted his car out in front of Edwina's house, parked the night before at a drunken angle out from the curb. She banged on the back door and then gave up, and weaved her way among the pecan tree stumps to her own house where she called the sheriff. She waited in the kitchen of her house, staring out the window where Edwina's crooked body soaked up the first warmth of the sun. "Oh, those magnificent trees, those magnificent trees," Dottie sadly moaned.

Dottie had lived enough years to know death. Her own beloved Eugene had fallen dead in her own backyard, at a too-early age, and now she refused to go back over to

Edwina's, afraid that Death might still be in the neighborhood.

It took the EMS crew and Deputy Sheriff Billy Ray Warren working both ends of the house to finally rouse Reynolds at eight.

The doctor speculated Edwina died of exposure sometime in the hours before dawn. "Must have called out for help most of the night," he said. Reynolds sat on the sofa, his hands locked in front of him. The doctor looked down at Reynolds. "And you say you never heard a thing." Reynolds could only shake his throbbing head and look away.

Reynolds called Perry, got him at school. Then he called Sheila. He called Joy. He wished he had a God to call.

"Daddy's at his cabin, I guess," Perry said. Reynolds shrugged. By now Perry stood in the front room with Reynolds, neither of the brothers able to watch their mama's body being carried away. Neither of them able to cry. Reynolds could feel nothing but his own misery.

In the other room Beth sat at the kitchen table, going methodically through Edwina's phone book, calling Edwina's friends, calling Edwina's kin, calling Nashville and Vicksburg and Dallas and Houston. She asked Edwina's sister to let all the Scotts who lived across the river in the next county know she had passed on. There were too many for her to call, all the cousins of various remove, plus nephews and nieces, and widowed sisters-in-law.

Reynolds found an old pair of pull-on boots in the back of his closet and a jacket that was too small. Finding Ray Senior might not be easy, but he didn't want the sheriff or the Fish and Game boys to locate him, for them to be the ones to break the story to his daddy.

"How will you find Ray Senior?" Beth asked. She looked

up at Reynolds, then at Perry. She held her place in the address book with the eraser end of a pencil. Her eyes were wide and brown and not full of anger or accusations. Reynolds could have escaped into her eyes.

Perry looked at Reynolds, then back at Beth. "I don't know. I guess I'll pull my boat out to the marina. Red Tyner probably has a pretty good idea where Daddy's cabin is."

"I'll go with you," Reynolds said. "I guess." He was willing to do anything, go anywhere—even with Perry—to escape that house. But even as he spoke, he knew leaving would do no good, that he couldn't leave himself behind.

Perry drove. They circled by his house and picked up the boat. On the way back through town Perry slowed at the Donut Palace. He glanced at his brother. "Let's take a sack of donuts to the old man," Perry said and wheeled into the drive-through.

A peace offering, Reynolds figured, Perry always trying to find some way to make things right. On the surface, anyway, and always for show, Reynolds suspected. He felt woozy, needed some coffee, could use a donut himself, a sugar rush to get his head clear.

The brothers rode silently on through town, holding Styrofoam cups of coffee until they cooled. Reynolds licked the ends of his fingers after downing a couple of cinnamon twists.

Reynolds wasn't about to take the blame for Edwina dying this way. There were too many extenuating circumstances. There was the weather, the freeze during the night. On a warmer night, with the bedroom window open, Reynolds would have heard his mama. But on a warmer night, he admitted, no ice would have covered the steps.

And even if it had been warm Reynolds would have

turned on the window unit to cool the stuffy room, and it made such a roar Reynolds couldn't have heard a 737 landing next door.

Or if Joy hadn't been such a slut, catting around town, coming in late, insisting that Deanie stay there in the trailer, then Reynolds would have been in his own bed that night; or if his trailer was a house, a real house, with two or three bedrooms, then Deanie could have stayed for a while, and none of this would have happened. If, if, if. Reynolds' entire life was filled with those damned ifs, damned mistakes, damned regrets.

Through town now, Perry speeded up, the pickup rolling across mostly open country, the boat and trailer bouncing behind. This wasn't easy country, even in the spring and summer the softness of the sandy land and the verdant growth could fool you, hide the chiggers and fire ants and wasps and snakes. And now, in winter, the landscape stretched gray before them, leafless trees and bare pastures and rutted cow paths leading to rusted tin sheds that held stacked bales of hay.

They passed a clump of trailers on the left, the graded road of a new subdivision on the right. A herd of skinny brindle cows nibbled at the dead weeds of a fence line. But somehow Reynolds felt better now. The bleakness of the winter land inexplicably gave his spirits a strange lift. Or maybe it was the sugar and caffeine working together.

Perry looked over at Reynolds. "You were there all night," Perry finally said. "That's what the sheriff said, what Dottie told me."

"Yeah," Reynolds said, "and I didn't hear a goddamn thing." He shifted in his seat, crumpled the empty coffee cup in his hand, glanced around and tossed it to the floor in front of him. "It's as simple as this. I got a little drunk, slept hard, and wouldn't have heard a train hauling ass through the front room. Okay?" Reynolds wanted to say he was sorry. God he was sorry, but there was too much to be sorry for.

"I just asked," Perry said. "I'm not necessarily blaming you."

"Well, everybody else is. But how do they know what happened. Maybe she hit her head when she fell, was unconscious the whole time, died in her sleep without ever making a sound. How do they know she cried out for help?"

Perry nodded, looked straight ahead as he drove. "Mama was a good Christian woman," he finally said. "We have that for consolation, anyway."

"Shit," Reynolds said. "That may be consolation, but it's yours. Not mine."

"It could be, you know," Perry said, "if you'd give yourself over to the Lord, give up your . . .well, you know, change the ways of your life."

"Ways of my life?" Reynolds said. "Now what the hell kind of talk is that? Have you forgot everything you knew, does that goddamn, tight-assed little let's-pretend church even ruin the way you talk? What you mean is give up drinking whiskey, chasing after strange women. `Ways of my life.'" Reynolds shook his head. "Shit."

Perry frowned, but he did seem to be listening—impatiently. Reynolds could tell that Perry was eager to repudiate him, ready to counter everything that Reynolds could say even before he could say it. Reynolds could feel his brother's arguments and counter-arguments and self-righteousness fill the pickup until he thought they might all explode.

They rattled across the causeway and Reynolds looked out to his left beyond Perry, beyond the shallow inlet of Clear

Creek Lake, and tried to envision being back at his place, just five or six miles south by boat, snuggling up next to Joy. How many times had Reynolds wanted to pull time backwards, to erase some disaster as if it had never happened? He suffered from time-sickness, his life no more than a catch pen of trapped regrets.

Around the next curve Perry slowed and in a couple of minutes he pulled the truck and trailer onto the rough parking area at the Red Top Store. Reynolds motioned for him to drive on around toward the marina, and Perry eased down nearer the lake. He circled, pulling out and away from the boat ramp and stopped. "We'd better check with old man Tyner," he said, his voice even, but tight with hidden anger. "I could only guess how to find Daddy's place."

Reynolds grunted his agreement, and opened the door.

Perry reached over and gripped Reynolds' arm. He had his beatific, holier-than-thou expression all over his face, and Reynolds sank inside. "Sometimes," Perry said, "actually always, it's good for a man's soul to cleanse himself, to repent of his sins."

Reynolds jerked his arm away, stepped out of the pickup and deliberately, gently, pushed the door shut. Just keep your cool, he told himself, and he tried to concentrate on screwing Joy or taking that first sip of Old Fitz, or Glenn Gould, lost in the flurry and gentle fury of Bach.

But when Perry came around the front of the truck, bouncing on his toes the way he did, with that pious smile still on his face, covering his anger, Reynolds exploded. "I guess you know repentance, don't you, little brother. Must take a shit pile of it when you've killed a man."

"What the.... Who told you that?" Perry glanced around and put a finger to his lips.

"I don't give a damn who hears me. You're a couple of quarts low on honesty. Repentance, my wore-out ass. You're the one who needs to come clean. You need a big sign, we'll put it right here, right on the side of your truck," and Reynolds pointed, gestured hard, "'Perry Dale Reynolds is a killer, but he does herewith and, and, so forth,'" Reynolds sputtered, "and he does duly repent."

The back door of the Red Top slammed right then and Red Tyner came out, carrying a five-gallon bucket of carcass trimmings. He nodded, straightened up, and wiped his hands on a bloody apron.

"Hey Red," Reynolds yelled, pointing to his brother. "Perry is a goddamn killer. Did you know that? Kicked out of the Marines, too. And there's a lot more, a whole lot more."

And then Perry charged his brother, hit him in the chest with his shoulder and Reynolds felt the air explode from his lungs. He hit the gravel hard, landing on his back, his head snapped hard against the ground. The last thing he remembered was Perry on him, straddled across his chest, both hands pressed over Reynolds' mouth, smothering his gasps for air.

TEN

RAY REYNOLDS SENIOR read by the glow of his kerosene lamp until the sun's first light filtered through the dense overhang of pecan and oak and hickory trees that sheltered his cabin. He read propped up on his single iron-framed bed, the lantern balanced on a twig table. He had built that table, put it together from limber willows that grew in one of the few clearings along the spring that had its source just up from his place. A tent of mosquito netting suspended from the plank ceiling hung loosely over the bed.

Every so often Ray marked a sentence, underlining it with a pencil he held in his hand as he moved slowly through the pages. Sometimes he circled a technical term that was new to him, then neatly printed it on a yellow pad he kept at his side. He had a whole string of strange terms he would look up in one of his reference books later. Often he went over a paragraph more than once, groaning sometimes in frustration when the accumulation of words just didn't make sense. This was heavy going for Ray Senior, but the answer was within his reach, he knew. Finally, he had perpetual motion by the *cojones*—the theory at least.

He glanced up from the page though, and his eyes traveled slowly over the dozen or so books and the worn volumes of *Popular Mechanics* that rested on a shelf across the room. Easier than when he started more than four years ago. He realized now that the answer would come—and it would come—not from a single flash of insight or discovery, but rather by taking this small piece from here, and another, almost incidental idea from there. The machine ran now while he read. The eighth day marked on his calendar, eight days that he had worked and slept and eaten while the stainless steel machine almost silently whirred and whished.

Ray's latest idea, the one with the most promise for him now, involved the creation of a Plexiglas vacuum to hold the machine. UPS should have delivered the materials he needed to the Red Top Store by now. He would pick them up later this morning.

Ray wore an undershirt and a pair of jogging pants that he had picked up at the Wal-Mart in Cottonwood. He stretched, moved his head gingerly from side to side.

Nights had become hard, sleep prowling around the cabin most of the night, taunting him like a miffed cat. Just before daylight he had lit the lamp, punched up the fire in the wood stove, as much for a feeling of comfort as for the warmth, and read until dawn.

Ray checked the calendar. December 15. He drew a line through the fourteenth. Three more months and I'll be seventy, he thought. "Seventy," he said aloud. "Old man, it's not going to get any easier."

He pulled on his windbreaker and ducked through the low doorway. He stepped into some flip-flops that rested on the plank porch and moved a few feet to his right, his toes aching from the cold, the leaves crunching from a light frost that had coated them during the night. He stopped and pissed, the stream slow to start, then barely arcing, splattering sporadically on the carpet of leaves. He watched his shadow as he pissed, turning to profile his drooping penis. "Plumbing," he said. "Just goddamned plumbing. A goddamn drain. Not worth a damn even at that."

In the shadows of the morning Ray looked younger than sixty-nine, for in the short time here in the woods, miles from the nearest road, and many more from the nearest town, cutting firewood, eating squirrels or rabbits—whatever he could pick off with his twenty-two—Ray had trimmed down so much that he had stapled a tuck in his khaki trousers, one on each side, and punched two extra holes in his belt.

At first he had missed Cottonwood, the way he took off from the house early so he could catch his truck-buying prospects on their way into work. There was nothing quite like driving up to that familiar dealership, the early morning sun gleaming off the hoods of a couple of dozen Ford pickups lined up, noses out, facing the highway, the flutter of the banners strung every which way, all of those colors. Why, it was like a carnival there every day.

Ray missed his twice-a-day sessions at the Donut Palace; he missed Edwina's meatloaf and pot roast and gravy. Some days he even missed her. But she had been just another bad habit in his life, like the donuts and the rich food, and he was better off without them.

Now back inside the cabin he pulled his trousers on and

with a quick slice of his pocketknife took three inches off the dangling tongue of his belt. He shook off some feeling of dread he had waked with this morning and poured a couple of cups of water into an enamel pan. He would have his coffee here and wait until he got to the Red Top Store for a package of cinnamon rolls. His once-a-month treat.

He picked what seemed to be the cleaner of two shirts that hung from the ears of a chair, pulled it on, and tucked the shirt easily into his baggy pants. He shook his boots out, checking for spiders or scorpions, then pulled them on. All the while he thought about what he had read for the past two hours, not quite grasping the nuances, but getting closer. Maybe the new silicone lubricants would do the trick, at least measurably extend the motion of the machine.

It would make the headlines, at least in the Business Section of the Dallas News. "You're going to surprise lots of folks, old fellow," he said, his voice hard with vague resentment. He tapped his finger on the side of his head. "One hell of a lot more here than meets the eye."

Ray pulled himself straight, splashed some water from a tin basin onto his face, and rubbed at the corners of his eyes, the corners of his mouth. He still wanted to look good, as much as possible, and for an old man he did, although his skin hung wrinkled and thin on the backs of his hands and his scalp gleamed through the sparseness of his hair. "That's what caps are for," he said, and pulled on the "Ford Trucks" gimme cap he saved for his trips to the store. He checked himself in the muted reflection of the mirror.

Still not a bad looking fellow, he thought.

On a scrap of paper Ray made a list, checking the rat-proof jars of flour and sugar and corn meal on a shelf above the wood stove. He filled the lamps with kerosene and sat the almost empty can outside under the overhanging porch where he wouldn't forget it.

Ray stayed busy while he sipped his coffee. He secured the metal door on the wood stove and found his wallet, which he no longer carried every day. He pocketed his glasses, his pouch of tobacco, a packet of cigarette papers. He watched the machine, the spin of the wheels and gears, the silent swing of the counterweights. He listened to the magic of its purr. Maybe this is it, he thought, maybe it will go on forever this time. But in his heart he knew the machine still was flawed. Worse, he wondered if Edwina was right. Nothing is perpetual but God. Ray looked up, raised his fist in the air. "You old bastard," he said. "I'll show you."

Outside he stopped on the porch. There in the fresh morning air his own smells of woodstove smoke and sweat settled around him. Honest smells, he thought. But today there was something more intense about the smells, something indefinable that unsettled him just a little. "Not a damned beauty contest," he told himself. "Just a trip to the store."

He picked up the empty kerosene can, checked his coat pocket for the shopping list, and moved toward an opening in the woods. Ray followed the narrow trail east the half mile from his cabin to the lake, and at last broke out of the tangle of briars and vines that now, in the winter, had pulled back from the path.

There, the north end of Clear Creek Lake opened up before him. The beach of baked mud wouldn't impress the folks who traveled the six hours south to Padre Island, but Ray Senior always felt a little rush of excitement when he reached the shore of the murky lake. The breeze out of the northwest had picked up in the last hour, and now tiny whitecaps fluttered in irregular lines across the water.

Ray set the five-gallon can to one side. Already he dreaded the coming back, the round can heavy with his monthly supply of kerosene, plus a box of groceries, plus whatever UPS had for him. It would be warmer by then, he figured, but he would have to make two trips back over the trail to his cabin, and all of a sudden he felt old, older than sixty-nine, older than God. Or the Devil. Ray snorted. "As if either one of you old farts exist."

He stared out over the lake for a minute, shading his eyes from the morning sun. Then he bent over, his hands resting on his knees, his breath still short and shallow.

"Those damned cigarettes," he said out loud. "Too late to stop now." Despite the frigid air a few drops of sweat dripped from the stubble on his chin to the gray soil below.

Ray Senior tried to read some sense into the pattern they made, the way a fortune teller might read a random scattering of tea leaves. But he couldn't.

Ray straightened up and made his way toward the water's edge where his boat rested half in and half out of the water. He picked his way across the dry mud flats, stepping around miniature towers of crawfish mounds. He kicked at a row of driftwood, scattering the wood with a mix of plastic scraps and a couple of faded beer cans. The driftwood still followed the curve of the lake where the lake level had reached its high-water mark in the spring.

Ray Senior eased himself down, resting for a moment on the bow of the boat. He pulled the pouch of loose tobacco and a packet of papers from his shirt. He rolled a cigarette with one hand, licking the edge of the paper, feeling the cracked dryness of his fingers. He scratched a kitchen match across his belt buckle and lit up, and after a couple of drags he felt better.

The boat, a fourteen-foot johnboat, collected a little water in its stern and Ray hadn't figured out if the slow accumulation came from a tiny leak or was simply rainwater that hadn't quite evaporated. He only used the boat once a month or so, especially in the winter when he didn't care to fish, but always at the middle of the month, after his social security check would be at the store.

While he rested he pulled a list from his top pocket and checked each item off in his mind:

> check mail
> ten # pinto beans
> Crisco
> cornmeal
> Vienna sausage
> sardines
> tobacco
> crackers
> hot sauce
> aspirin
> mail $ to Edwina

Ray glanced down the lake where a couple of fishermen in a fancy bass boat were trolling. One of them gave him a nod, a little wave. Ray ignored him. "Too damned cold to fish," he said. Must be a couple of fools, he thought. Like me.

He looked past the men and their boat, following the lake until it narrowed and disappeared between two sandy hills. The lake opened up again, he knew, to the south past those deep narrows, and in another six or seven miles the water would lick against a concrete boat ramp on the beach below his oldest son's liquor store.

"Bad enough to be a banker," Ray muttered. "Worse to be a failed one. But now a liquor store." After a couple of months out here alone, talking to himself didn't seem odd at all. Ray shook his head, took off his cap for a minute, wiped the sweatband on the knee of his khaki pants. He flicked the stub of his cigarette into the water and watched a school of minnows dart around it.

For a minute he concentrated across the lake, honing in on the red roof of the store that shined dully in the morning sun. Even from that distance Ray could make out a few boats in the marina and several cars in the parking lot. He hoped things wouldn't clear out too much before he got over there. "Goddamn Red Tyner," he said. "He says another word about Junior and that damned liquor store and I'll wipe that grin off his face."

Two months ago Red Tyner had waited while Ray Senior shopped, picked up his cans of Wolf Brand Chili and pouches of Bull Durham and on and on—damned near forty dollars worth in all. Red had waited until Ray went out to the pump and filled the can with kerosene, waited while Ray checked the boxes of .22 longs and the brass fishing hooks and picked up a bundle of rope and an overpriced box of nails. "Yeah, you waited, you miserly son of a bitch, waited until I had paid for everything, had dropped the money order to Edwina in the mail slot."

"Hear your boy's got hisself a real business going now," Red had said. "A liquor store." He waited for Ray to say something, and when he didn't, Red kept on, his words slow and measured as if he had been practicing all month, waiting for Ray to come in. "Hear he's got a new woman, too. That Boyd girl, the middle one." While he talked, Red straightened up the rows of candy in a rack. He was half-turned from Ray, but Ray could see Red's ears and the shiny top of his head, the way they began to glow when Red got excited.

"Yeah that Joy Nell Boyd, I hear she's a ringer. Least that's what her first two husbands said. Or was it three? Yeah, her and Junior, the two of 'em, shacked up in that wore-out trailer out back of the liquor store. Makes you wonder how far a man can slide before he busts his butt."

"Son of a bitch," Ray had muttered, while Red grinned.

And now, staring out over the lake at the Red Top Store and Marina once again, Ray repeated himself. "Son of a bitch," and shook his fist at the distant store.

Ray Senior worried about his talk with Reynolds, worried that he had told his oldest son too much about Perry. Now his two boys would be farther apart than ever. Letting go of Perry's secret had been just one more thing to escape from, another in the long line of reasons he had high-tailed it out of there. The boys had to own up to their own lives. A man did well to rope and throw his own problems, without chasing after all the others.

Ray unlocked the chain from the ring on the boat's stern and secured the kerosene tank between two seats. He rolled the cuffs of his pants to his knees and he leaned backwards against the boat, pushing and rocking it side to side until it began to slide easily. Just before the boat bobbed out onto the lake, Ray eased himself aboard and in a half-crouch made his way to the back seat. While the boat gently rocked, he checked the fuel in the engine, choking it, giving the starter cable a couple of good yanks. Then it took a half dozen more pulls before the little engine sputtered to life, and Ray turned the boat's nose toward the red-roofed building across the way.

Cranking the motor had not been easy. "Took the damned

starch out of me," Ray muttered, and he felt his right arm limp, aching, almost useless at his side. "How long can you do this, old boy?" he asked himself, and he thought about Edwina, twenty miles away, puttering around in her little frame house. For a moment he felt a longing for a real house, a home where his boys could stop by, and Junior's twins could visit from West Texas and Perry's girl could spend Saturday nights while Perry and Beth went to a movie or played forty-two with their friends.

Then Ray transported himself back to that house that he and Edwina had shared for more than forty-five years, where they had raised the two boys. The narrow concrete walk out front flanked by patches of iris and zinnias, the flowerbeds now mostly overrun with Bermuda grass. The house itself, when they had built it just after the war, was quite respectable, something to be proud of for a man who had started the year before selling Ford pickups for the only car dealer then in town. And Ray Reynolds could sell Ford trucks. He loved Ford trucks, the new smell, the smoothness of their bodies, the new models each year, always with improvements—more power, better mileage, seats you could ride on all day—the only thing that got better and better as time went on. Edwina hadn't, for sure.

And now, almost in mid-lake, familiar smells blew across him from the east, as if the breeze had passed over and through the frame house at 604 Prairie Street and whipped his way those smells of bacon grease and coffee, mixed with mold from the wooden floors. Not too bad. But then he caught a whiff of Edwina's powder and cold cream and the overpowering sweetness of the potpourri spilling out of little china knick-knacks everywhere you turned. There had been only one way to escape that.

But still he pictured himself there, finally retired from peddling pickups to would-be cowboys and roofers and insurance salesmen. And what was there to do? Sneak out back to the shed to work on his machine, putting up with Edwina, the way she put him down for his invention. What else? Watch Edwina cook. Watch Edwina read her bible twice a day, morning and night. Listen to Edwina talk back to Dan Rather.

Was that a life? Selling Ford pickups for forty years was not dishonorable, not the way that Ray Senior had done it, but is that what life came down to? And to live the last of your days with Madam Queen, who had for her own reasons grown narrow and bitter with disappointment? Did Ray Senior have to resign himself to that? "Hell, no," he answered now.

But this wasn't perfect either, living alone, living the life of a hermit, most folks would observe. But after only three months he had gotten to know himself, know who Ray Reynolds was, how he fit into the world in some small way. His machine would save him. Not Madam Queen and not his boys, who would do well to save themselves—and not his grandkids or Ford pickups. His salvation was his perpetual motion machine. "Hallelujah, amen," he shouted and gunned the boat's little motor to full speed.

When he neared the Red Top, Ray slowed the boat to an easy glide. There was a crowd of folks around the boat landing, a half dozen or so, and Ray Senior figured somebody had caught a big string of bass, or maybe somebody had drowned. But he didn't see an ambulance or a deputy sheriff so he figured it was no big problem. He cut the motor on the boat as he slid past the boat stalls and bumped the stern onto the narrow strip of beach below the store.

He stood up in the boat and he could make out a couple of men scuffling, tumbling around on the ground. And there, right in the middle of things, Red Tyner stood, legs spraddled wide apart, wiping his hands on his bloody apron. He spotted Ray Senior, waved for him to come on in a hurry. Red had a big grin on his face like there was something that he couldn't wait for Ray Senior to see.

ELEVEN

TWO DAYS later, almost noon on the day before his mama's funeral, Reynolds wandered out of her overheated house into the cold dampness of the backyard. Little piles of last year's leaves and rotted pecans were everywhere, a roll of black plastic sacks and a rake leaned up against the back fence. Life goes along with its mindless shit, Reynolds thought, and just like that it's gone. He kicked a pile of leaves left behind after the pecan trees had been sawed up and carted off. He could have sacked those up for his mama, but instead he always had come and gone like her house was a damned motel, sleeping in his old bed, letting Edwina fry his eggs.

And now she was dead. Gone.

Reynolds stood beside a flower garden, breathing easy, his chest still sore where Perry had banged him with his shoulder. From there Reynolds could observe the house, and for the first time ever noticed what time had done, the way the siding rotted where it met the ground, the way the white paint mildewed around the eaves. The curl of faded shingles rippled down the roof. The house he had grown up in had never seemed so small. The steps to the back porch this morning gleamed dry and smooth. They had been coated, slick with ice just three nights before. The thought made him angry, and he fought with an almost uncontrollable urge to burn the house down.

Inside the house gathered mostly forgotten kin, the Scott clan, his mother's people, some from as far away as Vicksburg and Nashville, but most from thirty miles to the west, just across the river where his mother had grown up. Reynolds had escaped the house to be alone in the backyard, escaped the smells of green-bean casseroles and buckets of Kentucky Fried Chicken, escaped the furtive glances, the sympathetic shakes of the head. Good people, well-intentioned people. They had all gathered. They all blamed Reynolds for Edwina's death. He guessed they were right.

The back door slammed and Reynolds didn't turn, didn't give a damn who in the hell it might be. But he heard footsteps coming his way, stopping next to him. "You want to go with me and Beth to see Mama?" It was Perry. Still being the good brother. After Reynolds had recovered from their scuffle out at the Red Top Store they had talked, he and Perry, while a doctor in town put five stitches in the back of Reynolds' head, and checked for cracked ribs.

The fight had cooled them both down for the time being, and a lot of their anger got detoured to Red Tyner when he blurted out to Ray Senior that Edwina had "fell and expired on the spot, with your boy in the house not fifteen feet away, dead drunk asleep."

All Reynolds could remember about those few moments was a groggy recollection of Ray Senior repeating over and over in disbelief that "Madam Queen is dead, Madam Queen is dead," until Perry managed to lure him into the pickup with the sack of donuts.

Without saying much at all the two boys called a truce, more uneasy than before. For years the old truce between them had been mostly silent. Awkward and shaky and agitated, but not out in the open. Now this was more of a cease-fire than a peace treaty, agreed upon when they saw in a few moments what years of suppressed agitation could do.

"Beth went to the funeral home earlier. Said Mama looked fine, real natural. You have to give them credit, those McKinney brothers down there really know what they're doing."

Reynolds turned. He faced Perry but gazed past him, back at the house. It was already after noon. The funeral would be tomorrow morning. Reynolds hadn't even stopped by the funeral home to pay his resects to Edwina. The kin would work up a groin pull over that.

"Well, hell, Perry," Reynolds said with a quick glance at his brother, then back towards the house. He could tell Perry had been crying. "I've got to go back out to the lake, check on the store. Stick is watching things for me, and I need to make sure he's still able to make change." Reynolds forced an uneasy laugh. "Anyway, I need to check, see if I can still fit into my suit." Reynolds grinned. Perry didn't, just ran his fingers across the buzz cut of his hair.

Reynolds still looked straight out over his brother's head to the house as they talked. Through the screen of the back door Reynolds could see someone—some woman—watching them, and he figured it was Beth, keeping her eye on Perry, making sure her husband didn't pick up any of Reynolds' sinful habits.

"Well, okay," Perry said, "but Beth thought it would be

good if we all went together. You know, the two of us and you and your boys. It's the right thing to do you know."

"They've taken off somewhere," Reynolds said with a shrug. "The boys. They said they'd be back by one, but who knows?"

Perry glanced around as if he could sense Beth behind him. "Okay," he said. "Anyway, I tried." Perry's face flushed, and Reynolds could hear the angry edge in his voice. Reynolds flinched, figuring that Perry might flatten him again.

Reynolds tried to extrapolate this moment in some imaginary way back twenty years or so when Perry, in an act of what must have contained some of this same repressed rage, had struck and killed Mouth. It seemed so unlikely now, and so long ago, that Reynolds was no longer convinced that it had really ever happened.

"Maybe I'll stop by the funeral home on my way back into town, later," Reynolds said, "or spend some time there tonight."

But Perry was already halfway to the house, bouncing on his toes, his arms swinging, his head held high, as if he were back in the Marines.

"Well, shit," Reynolds muttered. He did have to go back to his trailer to check out his funeral suit, and Stick could hardly be trusted for more than half a day at a time. And it was true about Larry and Garry—the boys had scoped their grandmother's house, found it pretty dull, and had taken off, Reynolds figured, in search of more action.

Larry and Garry had driven into town from Odessa last night with Sheila, but he hadn't seen them until this morning when they came over to Edwina's house. Sheila wouldn't let them visit him at the trailer, partly because of Sheila's idea that trailers were for trailer trash only and partly because she worried that Joy would be there.

Reynolds felt awkward around his boys; they had changed so much in four years. Now, at seventeen, they were as tall as Reynolds and had seemed like stiff strangers when he gave them awkward hugs. They appeared foreign to him, in navy blue slacks and white shirts and clip-on ties and polished loafers. "Flat tops," Reynolds had said when they came in, "just like your old man."

The boys laughed and rocked back and forth in uneasiness.

Reynolds ran his hand through what was left of his combed-back hair. "I mean like it was in high school," and the twins stared at Reynolds as if he had suddenly stumbled on the scene from some ancient and not quite parallel universe.

They both had Sheila's blue eyes, but their eyes held something else, a furtiveness, an evasiveness that Reynolds sadly recognized as his own. He fought off a sinking feeling as best he could. "Hey, you guys need some money?" Reynolds asked, digging into his pocket, pulling out only a handful of coins and an empty silver dollar money clip. "Hey, guess I'd better stop by the bank machine later."

"Mama already gave us plenty," Larry said, and Garry nodded. "We'll be back by one. Do anything for you?"

Do anything for me? God, has it come to this? Reynolds thought. He shook his head, and the twins took off to wherever young men these days take off to. Reynolds no longer could even imagine.

Back at the trailer he showered and then in his jockey shorts ate ice cream from the carton, secretly hoping that Joy might show up. But she didn't.

The suit didn't fit—Reynolds knew it wouldn't—but it

still looked sharp, a three-hundred-dollar sharkskin suit left over from his banking days. It would work for a couple of hours if he zipped up and didn't button. His belt would hide the gap. And the suit coat was fine as long as he wore it open. No problem. His mama might have cared, but she was the only one, and she was gone. Maybe Sheila, but to hell with her, Reynolds thought.

About 8:00 he closed down the store. To hell with the law, to hell with the beer drinkers. He slipped a half pint of Makers Mark in his jacket pocket and cruised into town.

He pulled around to the side of the funeral home, and one of the McKinney brothers was at the door when he made his way up the steps and past the white columns that ran across the front porch.

Buddy McKinney insisted that Reynolds sign the guest book, and he did. Now he was official, if Perry or Dottie or anyone checked up on him, he would be documented.

Edwina lay in a white casket in the back room, dressed in some pink blouse that to Reynolds looked unfamiliar. Buddy McKinney was going on and on about how peaceful she looked, how natural, how Beth had picked out the blouse from Beall's Department Store just yesterday evening.

Reynolds leaned over, drawing close to his mama's body. The part in her hair was wrong, anybody who knew Edwina could see that. Should be in the middle. But she did look soft, at ease for once in her life, as if now it was okay for someone else to take charge. "It won't be me, Mama," Reynolds whispered, and kissed her lightly on the forehead.

A couple of kin dropped by later, their faces and names all mixed up for Reynolds, and all he could do was nod and accept their condolences, agreeing, when they said he must want to be alone.

At 9:30 he meandered across the street to an all-night Texaco for a cup of coffee to go. Reynolds had skipped supper and was starved, so he picked up a twin pack of chocolate cupcakes. He figured he would have the place to himself by now, would sit next to Edwina for a half hour more and then leave. He doctored up his coffee with a generous but responsible shot of whiskey and, using his teeth, tore into the package of cupcakes.

Just as he took his first bite Reynolds sensed someone behind him. "I thought I might catch you here late. When you figured nobody else would stop by. I know you, Ray Reynolds Junior!" And Sheila did, had him figured out now, just like always before.

"You shouldn't be eating in here," she scolded him, looking around for one of the McKinney boys who moved in and out like shadows. "What would people think? It doesn't show proper respect."

Reynolds choked down the rest of the first cupcake and stuck the other one in his jacket pocket. He couldn't talk for a minute, not until he had a sip of coffee.

"Damn, Sheila," he finally said, still swallowing, "it sure is good to see you." He meant it. Joy being gone and all this shit coming down, he needed somebody to be with, to talk to. "The boys come along?"

"Oh, they're out on the town," Sheila said with a toss of her head, giving her frosted hair a bounce. "They're staying over at Perry's. I think they like the way Jennie's coming along. The three of them went out God-knows-where in Beth's van."

"Well, sit down." Reynolds looked around. A sofa was on one wall. "You can tell me what's been coming down your trail."

"Damned little," she said, but did sit down. She was decent, told Reynolds right off how bad she felt about him losing his mama, and that she had heard the stories and didn't know "how in God's creation" anybody could blame him for Edwina's death. "They have a double digit IQ problem around here is all."

Reynolds shared his doctored up, cooled down coffee with Sheila. She made a face and grinned. "Good old Ma Folgers sure can warm you up on a cold night."

Reynolds laughed, the first time he'd laughed in a week.

By the time the Makers Mark was gone the world had righted itself somewhat. When Buddy McKinney slipped back in the room Reynolds was into his massage mode, trying to "locate and exterminate" a knot Sheila had just above one shoulder blade.

They walked to the back of the funeral home together, Sheila's new Volvo glistening in the yellow lights of the parking lot, pulled up close to Reynolds' Lincoln. "Pretty fancy car for herding your daddy's cows," Reynolds said, patting the smooth roof of the Volvo.

"Works fine taking my daddy's royalty checks to the bank," she laughed.

"Shit," Reynolds said, and Sheila touched his arm lightly. A touch of sadness and regret, Reynolds thought. He knew sadness and regret when he saw them. Tonight especially. He hated to have lost his mama this way.

Reynolds found his cigarettes and offered one to Sheila. She shook her head. He lit up.

"I quit," she said. "You still smoke?"

"Only when I drink," Reynolds said.

"That much," Sheila said with a laugh. She lightly licked her lips and her frosted lipstick gleamed.

They stopped for a minute next to Reynolds' car. While they stood there Sheila tore little strips of rotted vinyl off the top. "Hey, you're ruining my car," Reynolds said with a grin.

"This car was ruined ten years ago, Reynolds. Just like everything else. You got any more of that bourbon in this piece of junk you drive?"

"Not one fucking drop," he said. "But I know where there's an entire store of it." He spread his arms wide, then without thinking circled them around Sheila's waist and tried to draw her close.

"Uh-uh," she said, pushing him away. "You had your chance already, way back whenever."

"How did I do?" Reynolds asked. "On a scale of one to ten?"

"Uhmm," Sheila said, trying to think. "On a scale of one to ten, you did R."

"R? What the hell is R?"

"You did R," she repeated. "R for Reynolds." Sheila laughed, ducked into the Volvo, and with a smooth roar of the engine she was gone. The shiny car hurrying out into the Cottonwood, Texas, night.

"I did R," Reynolds said out loud, leaning against his Lincoln Town Car. "Shit, I always do R." He slid into his car, slumped down in the seat, and stayed there for a long time.

TWELVE

AFTER THE funeral Joy had the decency to move out without any hassle, so Reynolds got his trailer back. Ray Senior right away listed the house in town with Century 21 and retreated back to his place on the lake. "You can stay there until it sells," his daddy told him. But Reynolds turned him down, hoped never to go there again.

Joy was gone, but forgetting her wasn't all that easy. Weeks later, a long strand of brown hair from her ponytail would turn up on the bathroom floor, or the smell of her shampoo would suddenly drift through the tight air of the trailer, startling Reynolds.

Reynolds missed waiting for her and found himself after hours still watching the bridge across the lake for her one-eyed Dodge Dart. But he wanted her out of his life, so he could move on—and up, he hoped. He had loaned her fifty bucks when she left and figured that was a pretty safe way to insure he wouldn't see her again.

The January days uncoiled slowly, Reynolds mostly scrabbling by with just enough business to keep the doors open, doing the dirty work of taking inventory, figuring his last year's taxes. Once in a manic fit he Murphy-soaped the store's wooden floors, then waxed and polished them.

One Monday Reynolds had just got some new music, the Kronos Quartet playing a bunch of tangos—he'd come upon a music review in Time and sent for the CD right away. This turned out to be music to move to, and even though it was afternoon, he turned the volume up, slipped out of his loafers and began to move around the slick floor in his socked feet.

He had slid around the back corner of the middle aisle, careful not to bump a promo display of cheap tequila, when he saw a reflection in the beer cooler, someone at the door. Shit. He'd been caught dancing. He bent over to catch his breath, then pretended to check some bottles on the bottom shelf before he straightened up again.

"Don't let me stop you," a woman said.

Reynolds felt himself flush. He nodded. "Come on in, come on in. Just getting some cardiovascular, you know."

The woman moved towards him. The door at her back with its light made her difficult for him to see, but as she got closer, Reynolds became more interested. This was not a regular, but a strange woman, one who dressed like some young kid, her jeans with a hole at one knee, and she wore a loose Mexican blouse with flowers embroidered across the top. Her hair was curly, really frizzy, black as hot asphalt, dyed, Reynolds guessed. It was shoulder length and stuck out every which way and bounced when she walked. She had a scarf looped behind her neck and tied on top of her head. The scarf was bright, yellow and pink and blue, the colors of a Nuevo Laredo market.

"In Cottonwood they told me you might have some

decent wines. Either here or I'd have to drive up to Dallas. Sure don't want to do that."

She stepped towards Reynolds then and extended her hand. "I'm Natalie," she said. He took her hand, and her skin was hard, calloused. The only other woman he had known with a right hand like that was a bar gal he dated a few times. Her hands were tougher than a hog's snout from twisting the tops off of longneck beers.

"Reynolds," he said with a nod.

"That's all?" she grinned. "Well, I sure hope your wine's as good as your music. Kronos Quartet? I think I'm gonna die sometime, trying to get away from those nasal Nashville boys."

Reynolds laughed. "Well, maybe it's you that's out of place. Anyway, I have a few good wines—don't touch the stuff myself."

"Too pricey?"

"Too slow."

"Well, I'll have a look-see," Natalie said, with a laugh. She had pretty white teeth, a good strong smile. Reynolds liked the easy way she laughed. She walked past him and her breasts bounced a little under the loose blouse. A good sign.

"You'll have to dust 'em off so you can read the labels. I just keep a few bottles around for show, letting them age, I guess."

In a little while Natalie brought a couple of bottles of Stag's Leap pinot noir to the counter. Reynolds wiped the bottles down, sacked them separately in slender sacks, and eased them together in a brown bag. "Can't be too careful," he said. "You from around here?" he asked. "I mean, if you don't mind me asking."

"North of town. Cottonwood. Yeah, I'm from around

here. For now." Natalie looked around the store, taking things in. Her eyes were brown and deep, they flashed when she talked, and her talk overflowed with energy, curiosity.

Now in the light, Reynolds could see she had some miles on her. They showed in the lines around her neck, the web of wrinkles that patterned the backs of her hands; her hips probably wider than when she was younger. Reynolds guessed thirty-eight to forty-two. Older than Joy by ten years or more, but Joy had been too young. Natalie had a self-assurance about her, obviously was sophisticated enough to know her music, her wine. Reynolds, he thought to himself, you'd better watch it. You may have met your match.

Natalie paid, took the top of the sack, folded it over carefully. She looked at Reynolds. "What's your sign?" she asked.

Oh, fuck, Reynolds thought, one of those moon-watching stargazers. He couldn't stand all of that New Age crap. But, as they say, a good woman. . . . . He pulled himself to attention. "My sign?" he asked, and held his right arm high, his two fingers in the Boy Scout sign. "I promise to do my best, to do my duty. . . ." He laughed.

"No, not that." She leaned over and touched his arm lightly. "Really now, when were you born?"

"May 24, in some untold year of our Lord."

"Oh, shit," she said. "Another Gemini."

"Something wrong with that?" Reynolds asked.

"Not necessarily, I guess. But I've known more than one, and they seem to have their tendencies."

A car pulled in out front, and although the parking lot was practically empty, edged in next to Natalie's vehicle, an over-sized GMC pickup. "Don't you scratch my truck," she said, shaking her finger towards the plate glass window.

"Sure is plenty of pickup for a little lady," Reynolds said.

"Woman," Natalie said, her voice bristly. Then she laughed again. "Don't call me a lady." She picked up the sack of wine and turned to go.

"Hey," Reynolds said, "let me know how you like that wine. Maybe I should order some more."

She stopped and turned again, looking straight at Reynolds. "Why don't you come out to see my operation— it's out on the Jacksonville highway. There's a sign— Wildspring Herb Farm. On the left about six miles. Maybe you can bring something new for me to sample. Something exotic if you can find it. Kiwi wine, maybe, from Australia. Something like that."

"It will have to be Sunday. Closed out here on Sundays only."

"Sunday afternoon then. I'll read your horoscope," she said, and Reynolds shook his head, raised his hand once again in the two-fingered Boy Scout salute.

The door opened and a couple of fellows waltzed in, moving quickly past Natalie, full of talk. They were young, cocky, and thirsty all at once. They turned while they walked, looking back to check Natalie out, then headed to the beer cooler in the back of the store. Reynolds would card them, slow them down just a hair.

"They know a pretty lady when they see one," Reynolds said with a grin.

"I have a sign for you," Natalie said, and it's not a two-fingered one, either." But she laughed when she said it, and then she was gone, hurrying out, the open door for a moment letting in a welcome rush of fresh air.

Reynolds did find a bottle of Kiwi wine by Sunday. He had to call Dallas and buy a case that he knew would mostly grow old on the shelf. Cost him $36 plus freight.

"You'd better be a special lady," he said to himself when he paid.

And she was, as it turned out. Sunday was a cold day, with first-week-of-February mist hanging in the gloom of the air. Reynolds eased his car through the narrow entrance, passing under the rainbow-shaped "Wildspring Herb Farm" sign and past the "Closed Until March 1" notice.

Right away Natalie took Reynolds for a tour of her greenhouse. There, the light was magnified in the convex and concave prisms of the place, and little rainbows sprang up in the fine spray of the misters.

Natalie had a place for the "mother plants," she called them—the perennial scented geraniums and salvias and thymes, the five varieties of oregano and lemon grass and seven kinds of rosemary. She showed Reynolds how she propagated the cuttings, dipping the tiny stems into the white chalky starter and tamping them into flats of soil. Already she had row after row of annuals that had sprung up from seed.

Reynolds was lost, as if he had entered into Natalie's own magic kingdom, but he found it fascinating—the smells of the soil and the fine mist in the air, the iridescence of the rainbows, the seclusion from the outside world, and the warmth.

The greenhouse was huge and packed with shelves of plants and flats. Natalie talked as they meandered through the place, intertwining an abbreviated story of her life while she worked. She wore a pair of cut-offs, had her hair tied back with a red ribbon, as best as could be managed, and wore another Mexican blouse, this one white, tied at the waist. A little sag of tan flesh worked its way over the top of her cut-off jeans, and when she bent over to work her blouse fell forward, exposing her breasts. She realized this, Reynolds knew, and knew also that she was the kind of woman who was neither an exhibitionist nor self-conscious. A natural woman, the first one Reynolds had been around in a long time, maybe ever. This was no North Dallas woman.

They stopped for a minute near the back of the greenhouse, where Natalie turned the heater's thermostat down.

"This is terrific," Reynolds said, "and you sell these plants, then?"

"Mostly by mail," she said, "I make up a little catalogue, sell seeds, dried herbs, fresh plants, some special potpourri I make up."

"A strange place to do this," Reynolds said. "Here in Cottonwood."

"Not really," she said. "Every place has their holys, you know, and their ass-holeys." She laughed and Reynolds nodded with a grin.

She had moved up from Austin, it turned out, with Circle, her daughter, and started the herb farm out here, mostly because the soil was rich and the land was cheap.

Austin had priced itself out of her market, with all the high-tech yuppies taking over the place. But for now her daughter had gone back to Austin, living with an aunt while she finished up school. "Circle hated it here," Natalie said. "You know how kids are. They can be cruel if you look or think a little bit off from the mainstream."

"Maincreek, around here," Reynolds said.

Natalie smiled, nodded, as if she liked his silly joke. It hadn't all been easy, she went on, and Reynolds listened, understanding why. East Texas is hospitable to lots of things—chicken fried steak and Republicans and Baptists, to name a few—but it's not herb-farm country. Especially if the herb farmer is female, goes around town braless in a halter top, (they'll sag down past her navel before long if she don't cinch 'em up, Stick speculated some weeks later). And more especially if she's a Libertarian, vegetarian, and indifferently vacillates between atheism (when she's pre-menstrual, she said) and agnosticism (most other times).

Around Cottonwood you were either in or you were out, Reynolds always said, but knew it was a lie. Natalie was out, but he was neither. Or, even worse, both.

Natalie dried roses and coreopsis and mint leaves and something purple and something else white and mixed it all together with a god-awful perfume of some sort, then packaged it in fake turn-of-the-century sorts of linen bags made from undyed natural cotton. Sold them for $5.95 each. Not big bucks, but enough so that over the next few weeks she could drive out to Reynolds' liquor store on the lake and buy whatever wine she damn well pleased. Natalie said she came out for the music Reynolds always had going, told him she would drive out there just to get away from the country classics the local station played over and over again.

Natalie was different from Joy, and not just the measure of a few years. She had drifted down to Austin not long after Reynolds had finished up at UT. She could remember the funkiness of the Jade Room, before urban renewal razed it, had waltzed across the sagging dance floor at the Split Rail, before it burned one sad night, and had even caught Roky Erickson and the Thirteenth Floor Elevators at the Vulcan Gaslight Company before those days ended in a haze of blue smoke.

Being with her, as it turned out, took Reynolds back to some good times, before marriage and divorce, before banking and going bust.

After a while Reynolds retrieved his cooler from the back seat of his Lincoln. He had brought the kiwi wine, and some wannabe microbrewery beers, all fancy labeled, but probably straight out of the Lone Star vat down in San Antonio, he guessed.

Natalie slid a cassette into her boom box, Gypsy airs of some kind, she told Reynolds, and they sipped the wine—a little sweet for Reynolds' taste—and sampled the beers. She started probing Reynolds, asking how he ended up out on the lake, but it turned out she knew most of it already. Reynolds eyed her suspiciously, accused her of being a witch of some kind.

"Not a witch," she said. "It's Dee, at the Donut Palace. She's my source for everything."

"Well, hell," Reynolds said, worried now how many lies Natalie had caught him in. "I went to high school with Dee."

"I know you did," Natalie said with a sly grin. "I know a lot. And it's okay. Not all bad. Dee says you're a little crusty on the outside, but soft in the middle. A cream-filled donut, she called you."

The Gypsy airs had run down to the end, and Natalie put on Knights in White Satin, the modern jazz quartet. She turned to Reynolds. "I could read your horoscope now," she said.

Reynolds groaned.

Natalie looked at him a minute, cocked her head to one side, thinking. Reynolds figured she was transforming into her stargazing mode.

"But," she said, her eyes suddenly glazed over mysteriously, "let's fuck, instead." She slipped her blouse up and over her head, and tossed it to one side.

"Right here?" Reynolds hesitated, looking around the

greenhouse, checking the clear glass door, but in a moment she was next to him, pulling at his shirt, unbuttoning it while she rose on her tiptoes to kiss him, her mouth soft and warm. Reynolds head filled with strange scents, Natalie's breasts pushed into his chest, and he concentrated hard to feel her nipples next to his skin, and then it was easy, Natalie laughing as she tripped stepping out of her cutoffs, and then her panties. In a moment Natalie was at his belt and moving on.

Reynolds gave a little moan, and they sank to their knees, both naked now, kneeling as if in prayerful gratitude on the spongy mulch, and Natalie pushed him backwards and down. Little beads of sweat broke out above her lip and her eyes closed, while above and behind her a rainbow formed and wavered in the mist of the still and pungent air.

❈ ❈ ❈

Reynolds came out to the herb farm most Sundays after that. Natalie would have her boom box going, always playing something strange or something old, some cello solo or a worn-out tape of The Band. Once some weird Tibetan Chant. Monk Grunting, Reynolds called it.

On one Sunday the weather had warmed, and already the elms were starting to bud out. Reynolds stood outside in the shadow of a shed for a while, watched Natalie move through her gardens, studied the way she bent and stretched, as if gardening had become a dance. What a waste he thought, gazing out over rows of lavender and statice. He imagined what she could do with a field of tomatoes and black-eyed peas.

Then he unfolded an old quilt, a Star of Texas pattern that had been his mother's, one that she had stitched by hand. He spread it in the shade, covering outgrowths of knobby tree roots and clumps of weeds, hoping the quilt would discourage the crawling critters. He settled onto the worn softness of the quilt and leaned back against the tree, rubbing his back lightly against the rough bark. He pulled a rumpled wad of bills and receipts from a paper sack and shuffled through them, making stacks on the quilt, securing each one with a rock. He held a calculator in his hand and stuck a red pencil behind one ear, but somehow didn't have the heart to start this weekly bookkeeping chore. Not yet.

He closed his eyes and fingered the frayed edge of the quilt. Just a couple of minutes, he thought. But every time he closed his eyes he saw his mama sprawled at the bottom of those icy steps, and if he didn't hum some nonsensical song—the Kinks' version of "Gloria" worked for right now—he could hear his mama crying out for help.

When Natalie took a break she joined Reynolds under the tree, sat cross-legged on the quilt, stretching this way and that, all the while humming something strange. "My mantra," she said. "Are you okay?"

Reynolds nodded. He wouldn't tell Natalie about his mama, the way she died. Not yet. She would hear it in town soon enough, he figured. If she hadn't already, from Dee. He sat up, tried to cross his legs the way Natalie did. But he was too stiff. "Yoga?" Reynolds asked, trying to shake things off. "Ohhmm," Natalie hummed, and nodded her head.

Reynolds had brought sandwiches. He could be a gentleman when he tried. For Natalie white Vermont cheddar, damned hard to find around Cottonwood and pricey as hell—he would let her know—with sprouts on nine-grain bread. A BLT on white for him. An Igloo with wine coolers (two sample, experimental flavors —Guava Strawberry and Hibiscus Cranberry), a couple cans of lemonade, and two

Elephant malt liquors he hoped Natalie wouldn't want. With his foot he pushed one of the stacks of receipts to the side, off the quilt. Three or four white curls of paper fluttered into the weeds. "Shit," he said to himself, but let them go.

He scooted closer to Natalie, ran his arm around her shoulder. Her skin was wet and slick with sunscreen and sweat. Smooth as a slip.

Natalie leaned close. She looked at Reynolds' sandwich and wrinkled up her nose. "You're taking your chances, you know," she said, "eating that bacon."

Reynolds held the ragged sandwich at arm's length. "Oink, oink," he said softly, and laughed. He took a bite.

Natalie pulled away. "Nitrates, nitrites, fats. God knows what else. Not to mention squealing, bleeding, dying pigs. I can't stand it."

Natalie studied her sandwich. "Even bread is beginning to bother me," she said. "I just don't know."

"Well, for sure I don't know," Reynolds said with a laugh. He chomped another big bite of his sandwich, dragged the last piece of mayonnaise-smeared bacon out with his teeth.

Natalie ignored him. "Well, you know that I bake my own bread," she said. "Whole wheat, rosemary bread, all that stuff. And I've been thinking." She gently waved a wasp away. "Did you ever make bread?"

Reynolds shook his head. He leaned forward intently, tried to show enthusiasm for whatever Natalie had come up with. But his heart still dragged along where he had left it a few minutes before.

"When you make bread, you add yeast to warm water. Right?"

"Right," Reynolds said, although he would have said right to anything.

"And then you add a little sugar, just a pinch, maybe. No more than a teaspoon for a couple of loaves. That's to proof the yeast, to make sure it's active, alive. If it foams, it is. Then you know your dough will rise. All those jillion little yeast bacteria all alive and working."

"Fascinating," Reynolds said, and Natalie glowered at him. "No, I mean it, keep going," he said. Reynolds, you're a shit, he thought.

Natalie opened her sandwich, extracted some cheese and sprouts from the bread and nibbled on them while she talked. "Okay. You shape your loaves, the yeast is still working like crazy, the loaves rise, and just like that you pop them into a four-hundred-degree oven. And what happens?"

"In thirty minutes you have bread," Reynolds said.

"Okay, but at what cost?"

Reynolds shrugged. "Beats me."

"You've killed all the yeast. They're dead. Gone forever." Natalie looked sad.

Reynolds could see that she was genuinely disturbed by this new awareness. Oh, shit, he thought. "Sad," he said, but with a laugh he couldn't fight off.

Natalie handed him the sandwich. "You just don't realize what you do, all you rednecks up here in East Texas. Killing and eating cows and pigs and shooting everything else that moves. You just don't understand how serious it all is, killing things, not being concerned with how it must feel."

She stood up. "I read a study where they wired up a red cabbage and then recorded the electrical impulses when they jerked it out of the ground. Its electrons and neutrons literally screamed."

Reynolds began to laugh, tried to stop, gasping "sorry, sorry," but he wasn't sorry at all. Or, yes, he was sorry, but not for Natalie and not for red cabbage and not for yeast. He tumbled out of control then, his laughter deep, roaring up from somewhere he had never known.

He still could see his mother, sprawled at the foot of the back-porch stairs, her fractured leg all aspraddle. He could hear the deputy sheriff, and Dottie Hairston, and Perry all asking, "How could you not have heard her?"

Reynolds rolled on his mother's quilt, his laughter now leaping out. Natalie backed away. Finally Reynolds stopped and gasped for air, but Natalie was gone, her figure only a ghost moving away from him through the greenhouse.

Women disappeared that way. Sheila and Joy already shadow women, going on about their lives as if Reynolds had not mattered one whit, as if all the romancing and screwing and dreaming and clawing and scrapping had slipped right off them without leaving a mark at all. And now Natalie.

Reynolds wanted to call out, wanted to tell Natalie that he was a sorry bastard for laughing. He needed to explain, to tell her that his laughter wasn't about what she said at all.

But why explain? Reynolds didn't give a damn about yeast, not dead or alive. "Bread is beginning to bother me?" He shook his head. "Jesus Christ. Who the hell wouldn't laugh?" He grabbed the quilt and the cooler. His Lincoln Town Car had never looked so good.

THIRTEEN

IT WAS almost six weeks after Edwina's funeral before Perry's source made contact again. He had begun to think the dealing might have run itself out, that he was too little a player for Skinny and his pals to mess with. Perry had been counting on the extra money, but inside he had started to feel an easiness that he hadn't felt for a long time.

So on Sunday night when his pager beeped, Perry felt himself come alive in a way that bothered him, made him uncomfortable.

Perry returned the call from a pay phone at the Sack It and Pack It in town, putting one hand to his ear when a truck blatted by on the way to Dallas. The area code he dialed was 713, for Houston, the number unfamiliar, not one he had called before. But Perry knew who it would be even before Skinny answered. These fellows might be on the shady side, but they were pros, something Perry could respect.

"This Thursday, at 10:30, at the same place." Skinny spoke quickly, his voice even, without the Spanish lilt Perry had picked up in person. The order was straightforward, Skinny placing his gun order as if it were a couple of pizzas to go.

"But Thursday's too soon." Perry said. "I need a little more time. You fellows have to give me more notice." He felt buoyant when he talked like this. He needed to be more aggressive, more assertive. Perry would call the shots for a change. They needed him as much as he needed them. "And Friday is better," Perry continued, his voice low, but strong. "10:00 on Friday night at the same place works much better for me."

A car pulled up next to Perry's pickup, a fellow in his salesman suit got out, tucked his shirt in over his belly, and made a half-hearted, automatic gesture to button his jacket, but couldn't. He fished for a quarter and waited a few steps away for Perry to finish. Perry nodded towards the man and turned away while he talked, his voice now low and urgent. "And I need to know the price, how much you will pay. This is America, and here we have to know these things."

"Listen," the voice said. It was no longer Skinny, but a deeper voice. Perry tried to imagine Shadow taking the phone from Skinny. "Be there Thursday, 10:30, or it's adios, no mas deals. Comprende? You deliver the stuff. Good stuff. Mucho bang for the buck, as you Americanos say. And we treat you okay."

"Well, I guess it will be okay," Perry complained, "although sometimes you may have to compromise a little." But the phone clicked and went dead. "Bastards," Perry muttered, then he checked to see if the fellow waiting behind him could have heard. Perry turned, the phone still to his ear, now facing the chubby man who waited. He raised his voice and nodded his head. "Sure honey, I'll be there in a few minutes. I just wondered if you needed anything else from the store. Love you."

Perry hung up, checked the coin return. He nodded to the fellow. "It's all yours," he said with a smile. "Have a nice day," and Perry turned quickly away, bouncing as he moved to his car.

During the week Perry worked to shore up his life. He drafted a letter to the school superintendent explaining his teaching technique of creating student interest "by posing controversial questions, and taking arbitrary positions (even if those positions conflict with my own, deeply held and basic values) in order to stimulate debate on those principles which are elemental to political freedom in America."

This teaching method would prove itself by the end of the year, he went on, "but for the sake of concord and harmony he now would compromise this approach, not realizing that some of the students, and their parents, might take offense."

He continued with a mild apology, reassuring the superintendent that he only had the students' best interests in mind (which was true). Satisfied that this would confuse the old fart, he sealed the letter and dropped it in the inter-office mail.

Tuesday at lunch he phoned Snider, caught him at home, and set things up as usual—this Thursday, the boat landing down from the liquor store at nine. They would run the boat up the lake to the safe house and pick up their load. Perry would lay low around the boat ramp, waiting in the dark until Skinny and his pals showed up. Snider would retreat to his usual place across the bridge in case of trouble. "Be there on time," Perry warned him. "These are no-nonsense fellows. And be alone. No booze, no women. We have to run a tight ship."

"Just hang loose, Cap'n. Perry," Snider told him. "Just hang loose." Snider really fried Perry sometimes with his nonchalant laid-back attitude. Just one more reason to close these deals out.

❊ ❊ ❊

A late norther blew in from the Panhandle Thursday noon, and caught Perry at school in a short-sleeved shirt. By the time he got home a fine mix of sleet and rain had raced down through Dallas and across that part of East Texas.

Perry was tempted to call the Houston number and cancel out, but was afraid he'd lose what little credibility he had with Skinny and his pals. From the bedroom he made a quick call to Snider. "Green," he whispered. "All systems are go."

Snider laughed. "Don't worry Cap'n Perry, I'll be there."

Damn you, Perry thought, and silently hung up the receiver. This is serious business.

At 8:00 Perry simply left the house, eased out of the door without a word. Beth ignored him, never looked up from some curtains she was hemming. That's how it should be, he thought. This was his own business, and a man shouldn't have to ask permission from anyone.

He and Beth, it seemed, had silently agreed not to fight over this, and if he could pull off one more deal after this one, bag a big one, then the whole thing would die a gentle death all on its on. Beth would have a few nice things for the house and the yard, Perry would have a little emergency money set aside if things fell apart at school. Maybe he could pay down on a little piece of land, get the Farmers Credit Bureau to finance a few cows for him.

For Perry the whole militia idea had pretty well dissolved. There had been too much misinformed publicity in the papers and on TV, too many wacko soldiers out there, getting together and acting like the jerks they were. They ruined things for those who could have mounted a serious alternative to America's bastardized democracy. Perry's organization wouldn't have a chance at credibility in this atmosphere. He would wait. "Tranquilo," Snider would have said.

Perry hooked up his boat in the half-dark, then took the back streets through town, knowing that it would appear a little crazy to be pulling a bass boat to the lake in the middle of an ice storm. That was the down side, but once Perry got through town and on the road to Lake City there would be no one at all. He and Snider, along with Skinny and his pals, would have the boat landing all to themselves.

When Perry approached the bridge over the lake, his wipers had begun to slide a light frozen film across the windshield, and he slowed, worried that the bridge might be slick. Across the way he could make out the shadow of Snider's car pulled off to the side of the boat ramp. Snider was on time—a good omen.

Up the hill the liquor store lights were off. No overtime for Reynolds, Perry thought with a shake of his head. The trailer was dark, too. Hell, Perry figured, the place is so small that Reynolds wouldn't even need a light to find the bed. Someone over coffee at the Pitt Grill had told Perry that Reynolds might be having woman problems—again—that the Boyd girl who lived with him was seeing someone else. Stories like that went around in Cottonwood, though, and true or not, Perry gave them little weight.

Honestly, he didn't give a damn about Reynolds' shenanigans. There had been one thing after another for so many years, with the bust at the bank, then the scandal of Reynolds' near indictment, and the divorce from Sheila. No wonder Ray Senior had taken off for the woods, no wonder Edwina had hardly ever left her house except to go to church. Bless her cranky soul.

Reynolds stream of problems didn't bother Perry, though. He was his own man, had his own reputation to fall back on, his high school football credentials—no small accomplishment—and then a degree from a more-than-decent college, marrying Beth, who might be a little dull, but was from an upright family, her father a pharmacist with an unblemished reputation.

They owned a nice house in the country, the mortgage would be paid off in twelve more years, sooner if things worked out the way he planned. That damned mistake in the Marines was his only stumble, and that was not his fault. A man must defend himself at all costs. The Marines, more than anyone else, should have understood that. They owed him, and he would not let it pass this easily. They owed him his benefits and owed him for his bad knees. Owed him his reputation.

Perry clicked the car lights down as he approached the end of the bridge and eased off the road onto the smattering of gravel that led down to the boat ramp. He flashed his lights bright once to orient himself and to signal Snider. Then he turned them off completely. In a moment Snider eased out of his car and guided him as Perry backed the boat towards the ramp. This would be easy.

By 10:00 the two men had finished their run to the safe house and had made their way back to the boat ramp, the johnboat riding low in the water with its load. They dragged the boat onto the trailer, Snider sipping from a beer the whole time.

When Snider drove off to take up his lookout position back across the bridge Perry pulled the pickup around, circled so that when he stopped he faced the hill towards the road. This way he could make a quick exit if there was trouble. He cut the engine, and for a moment listened as the sleet ticked against his windshield.

From there Perry could watch not only the road and the entrance to the boat ramp, but by looking out to his left could keep an eye on Snider and spot any car that topped the hill coming from Cottonwood, approaching the bridge. Lake City Liquors loomed in the dark above him, and even through the mist and sleet the place glowed dimly with the yellow-blue luster from the scattering of beer signs inside the store.

Just then Snider flashed his lights twice from across the bridge, his signal that he was in place. Perry wished he could be a little more like Snider sometimes. Snider never seemed to be broke or worrying about deadlines. If he had woman problems he simply got a new one. He would never consider looking back. Perry was certain that Snider couldn't spell introspection, had never heard of regret. He sighed. Nothing to do now but wait.

❈ ❈ ❈

This was a miserable night for Reynolds. At eight he locked the front door, slid the dead bolt shut, and hit the lights. A few cold weather, hard-hitting whiskey drinkers had stopped by early, stocking up, afraid they'd get iced in by the late winter storm. But for the last hour, from 7:00 to 8:00, there had been nothing, and Reynolds felt relieved to give up on this god-forsaken night.

With a bourbon in one hand, Reynolds backed up to the

space heater in the front of the store. In spite of his best intentions, he thought about Joy. She had been gone for more than two months now, and Deanie had ended up back with Joy's mama who had somehow worked things out. Joy hadn't made nursing school or even beauty school for the spring semester, but, from what he had heard, she was still working late shift at the Next to Nowhere. And he heard, also, that she had shacked up with a scrawny, pony-tailed pipeline welder in a trailer back in the flatwoods out south of town.

That was a big relief for the most part. Joy had gotten so independent those last weeks, unhappy with everything, it seemed—the way Reynolds talked, the music he played, what she could find in the trailer's half-size refrigerator. Sex didn't interest her anymore, Reynolds could tell, although they screwed regularly. But that was it, screwing, and had nothing to do with passion or caring. Just a couple of overgrown organisms humping in the dark, clinging together in desperation against the night, eager for some escape, some release.

Since Joy left, Reynolds had devised a chart in his head, "The Sexual Response of Women—A History," he called it, a way to track female sexuality, as he had observed it, up until age forty-five.

Reynolds moved back to the counter, poured a splash more of bourbon. He eased down in the swivel chair and lit a cigarette.

At thirteen the girls were hot but ignorant, more curious than sexually mature. They were lost in the dark, operating out of vague, undefined itches—mostly unproductive—a time that Reynolds called "Early Exploration."

By eighteen they were still mostly ignorant but had become clever, now saw sex as something to be used for their own good—to get a man, have steady companionship, etc., or a way to have a kid, which would prove to the world that they truly had arrived as women. Any and all of the above led to mostly disastrous consequences. This time he called "The Establishment of Colonies."

By their mid-twenties, sex had gotten old hat, and either preoccupation with babies or the fear of another pregnancy kept them unenthusiastic about the joys of a tumble. This he labeled "The Defense of the Frontier."

In their early to mid-thirties, they became sexually aware, really for the first time. Their kids most likely old enough to be in school, their husbands into their work, and their female hormones telling them that their reproductive years might be ending just around the bend. Whether they had kids or never wanted kids, their hormones gave not one shit. The message was clear—this is your time to screw, and to make sure you screw in this twilight of reproductive possibility, you will be awakened to sexual pleasure. Not vague itching and desires, and wanting to be cuddled, but full-blown orgasmic clinches seemingly without limits. And besides, the message went on, you know your bodies now, and hey, it can be pleasurable. Take it while you can. And the women do, with a horny vengeance. "Manifest Destiny."

Pity the poor husband of sixteen years who has been flirting hopelessly with the twenty-year old secretary in the front office. He must now perform, not for his own pitiful pleasure, but learn to couple for prolonged periods while on his back, reciting his mantra, maybe Carl Yastremski's year-by-year batting averages, in order to last long enough for the female aggressor to finally collapse, shuddering across his now worthless body.

Then a slow decline sets in, and sex becomes the path to

closeness and security, interspersed—thanks to the fickleness of hormones and the hint of menopause over the horizon—with flashes of exuberant craziness. "Isolationism with an Occasional Skirmish."

The clinker in all of this, the asterisk at the end of The Theory is the proviso that all can go out the window at any moment, be turned sexually and metaphorically topsy-turvy by the introduction of even the possibility of a new sexual partner, especially one whose grunts and warts and tics and farts are romantically unfamiliar.

Reynolds sat there for a long time, tried to find something appropriately mournful to slip into the boom box, but found his comfort in the dark, the aloneness, and the smoothness of the whiskey.

Finally, Reynolds put on an old tape of "Bolero," a cassette that he had played so often over the years that the tape had stretched, and now the music dragged deeply for a minute before things caught in place. He slipped off his shoes, tested the smoothness of the floor, but the stove glowed with warmth and his drink was still half full, so he didn't move.

Finally Reynolds wandered to the window and watched the bridge, heard the sleet pelt the window, while he waited out of habit, but without hope, for Joy.

One more drink might help, and then to bed, he thought. He started to turn towards the counter, but just at that moment Reynolds saw, or thought he saw, through the dark-splatter of the night, the flash of car lights, twice, at the end of the bridge across the way.

For a moment he thought it might be Joy, with car trouble or something, trying to signal him, but there had been two headlights, he was sure, and Joy would never get around to replacing her bad one.

At 10:30 sharp a dark van slowed and dimmed its lights, then turned, angling down the incline to where Perry waited. The same routine then. By the time Skinny slipped lightly down from the van, Perry had the tarp off the boat. Without a word Skinny and Perry started grabbing the guns, some of them with collapsible stocks and pistol grips, one bundle of Colt AR-15s, some Chinese SKSes. All shrink wrapped, two to a bundle.

"I'd feel better about this if I could have the price beforehand," Perry said. Skinny grunted and kept working, back and forth between the boat and the van. He made two trips to Perry's one. This fellow is all assholes and elbows, Perry thought, breathing hard, trying to keep up with Skinny's pace.

Suddenly, Snider's lights from across the bridge flashed on and off and on again, and almost simultaneously a car topped the hill behind Snider and approached the bridge.

Skinny and Perry both froze for a moment, and the van rocked a little as Shadow and Fat Hand shifted around. One of them said something quick and hard in Spanish, and Skinny glanced at the boat that still held another four or five bundles of guns and some boxes of ammunition.

Perry glanced at the car, and turned back to Skinny, "Hey, just take it easy, let's finish this up. I need my money." But at the same moment he noticed the approaching car slow after it had passed where Snider waited. Then it stopped.

No more than a few seconds later Snider spun his dark car out of the pull-off and with a rapid shifting of gears raced back up the hill towards Cottonwood.

In a moment the van started up, and Skinny leaped through the open sliding door and slid into the driver's seat.

The side door banged shut, and Perry could only yell, "Hey!" and dodge out of the way as the van roared up the hill.

Skinny hit his lights bright for just a moment so that he could be sure of the way towards the road, and then the van was dark again, weaving rapidly towards the hard surface at the top of the incline.

The car on the bridge backed up fast. Now Perry could hear the strained whine of its engine in reverse, as it wheeled backwards onto the pull-off Snider had just left. The car sat there a moment then, and Perry could imagine the driver, if it was a deputy sheriff or constable or whoever, deciding what to do. For almost certainly he had spotted the van in those few moments when Skinny flipped on his lights, desperate to find his way back up the hill in the overcast night.

Perry waited. He didn't dare open his pickup door for even a moment, knowing that the interior lights would give him away. So he stood there, shivering in the freezing drizzle, and watched. Sometimes you only can give yourself up to fate, to chance, he thought. Better to wait quietly and hope the bad passes you by than run straight into it.

The driver of the car across the way apparently had decided to let Snider go, and whipped back onto the bridge, accelerating after the van which had by now had screeched out onto the road above and raced in the opposite direction out of sight.

Perry watched the car roar towards him across the bridge, its headlights bouncing, and as it sped by he could see it wasn't a Shawnee County Sheriff's car, or the familiar black-and-white Ford of a state trooper, but a light-colored sedan with no markings. At that moment, a pair of red lights popped on, not bubbles on the top, but flashing lights that were hidden in the front grill.

Undercover of some kind, Perry knew, and what kind didn't matter. The sedan picked up speed as it topped the hill and then was gone like a bad dream at daylight.

Perry waited a moment, then quickly slipped into the truck. He sat there, thinking, careful not to touch the brakes, not knowing if there would be another unmarked sedan nearby. Surely the message was already out, and backup help of some kind would not be far away.

In a couple of confused minutes Perry went over his choices. He could back the boat to the water and stash the rest of the load in his safe house, come back empty, hitch up the boat and head back home. But the odds of that going smoothly were laughably low. He couldn't leave his pickup and trailer there by the boat ramp. How would he explain being out on the lake on a night like this? Where would he have been, in the middle of a winter storm, and what would he have been doing? He hadn't even bothered to bring his fishing gear this time—the weather would have made that pretense absurd. And, anyway, that had been mostly for Beth, and now he had stopped even bothering with fooling her.

Or he could take off now and pull the boat back into Cottonwood, hope he wouldn't get stopped. And then? What would he do with the guns? Leave them in the boat out beside his carport while he taught school all day tomorrow? That option was risky, if not downright foolish.

Perry checked the road above him, then in the dark started the truck and slowly eased forward, the boat swaying behind him as he made his way up the rocky ground. He knew the boat ramp well enough not to use his headlights until he topped the gravel incline and made the turn back towards the bridge and home. Now on the asphalt road, the boat trailed easily behind, but Perry drove slowly. He had nowhere safe to go.

☒ ☒ ☒

If Gerald Kemp had not stopped by on that Saturday, Reynolds would have watched the goings-on below his window in his normal, somewhat bemused way. For the road that led from the wetness of Lake City to the dryness of Cottonwood was, as often as not, spotted with the small dramas of the drunk, and the not-so-drunk, and the soon-will-be-drunk drivers dodging the cruising patrol cars that found the road to be easy pickings for DWIs and speeders, and minors in possession.

A patrol car whizzing by either way, its lights flashing, normally provided only a brief distraction for Reynolds.

But Gerald Kemp had stopped by, and Reynolds, alerted to the possibilities that might be unfolding at the boat ramp below was more attuned, even with his third whiskey, and despite the final surging of Ravel's masterpiece spinning through the darkness of the store.

Reynolds watched at the window, saw Snider flash his lights in warning when the green sedan topped the hill behind him. He watched as the sedan slowed, and then stopped, saw Snider's Nova come to life and race away up the hill. Reynolds then saw car lights below him at the boat ramp—somehow he had not noticed anyone there before—and in a moment watched a van rock its cumbersome way up towards him, and then turn out on the road, burning rubber as it took off past the front of the liquor store.

Before Reynolds knew it, here came the green sedan, the red lights flashing on just before it drew even with the store, and then with a whoosh it, too, was gone. "Hell, that's Kemp, the ATF fellow," Reynolds whispered aloud. Then everything got quiet.

Still Reynolds didn't move, letting the music and the warmth from the heater and the glow from the bourbon flow through him. And in a few minutes, while Reynolds watched from the dark of the store, quietly, slowly, a darkened pickup pulling a small boat eased up the incline. At the crest of the hill the pickup hesitated a moment before turning left onto the road that led back towards Cottonwood. It coasted quietly down the road towards the bridge, then its lights flashed on.

If Gerald Kemp of the ATF hadn't been there, at that very window on that Saturday, studying the boat ramp from above, asking those questions, then in the dark Reynolds might not have realized that the man in the truck pulling the boat was his brother. But now he did. "Shit and God almighty damn, Perry. What have you done now?" was all that Reynolds could say.

The music had stopped by then and Reynolds didn't have the heart for more. Not now, with Perry in this trouble of some kind. Maybe he should drive into town, go out to Perry's house and find out what the hell was coming down. Maybe he could help out. But then he thought, Perry never volunteered a goddamn thing when I was going through my troubles, in fact he hid out, ran the other way. And Perry was a shit when Edwina died, not taking up for me at all, cracking my head open and damn near busting my ribs.

Reynolds moved to the counter, snapped off the boom box, and found his jacket. But suddenly headlights moved across the back wall of the store and Reynolds froze. If it's that damned Kemp fellow, he thought, I'll just stay put. Won't go to the door. No crime in that, he figured.

But he eased into the shadow of a corner and watched, and the vehicle didn't stop out front but kept coming, pulled along side the store and kept going. It was not a car at all, but a truck, Perry's pickup, the boat still rattling along behind on its trailer.

By the time Reynolds slipped back into his shoes and pulled on his jacket Perry had pulled the truck around behind Reynolds' trailer, just scraping up against the rusted barrel where Reynolds burned his trash. When Reynolds opened the store's back door, Perry was already across the way, beating with his fist on the trailer door.

"Over here, brother," Reynolds said, holding the door open with one hand, and in a moment Perry was inside the store.

"I've got a load of trouble back there," Perry said right off the mark. "You need to know that. It won't be there long, one way or the other, but right now it's your trouble, too. If you want me to get the hell out of here, let me know, and I'll go. It's no problem of yours unless I stay."

Shit, Reynolds thought. Just what I need is more goddamn trouble. In the dim light cast by the beer signs and the gas heater Perry's one pale green eye washed completely out, and Reynolds found himself drawn in, lost in exploring its depth. Perry looked up at him, defiant and at the same time needing his brother. Reynolds might as well have been thirteen again and Perry six. Perry wet, shrunken, now beaten down. The sureness and the cockiness gone.

"What the hell have you got back there? Shit, Perry, I can't take any more trouble. I'm filled up, my tanks are overflowing."

Perry sagged some more. He started for the back door.

"Oh, hell," Reynolds said. "Hold on. It doesn't matter. You can stay. A load of trouble is nothing new for me. Hell, you're my brother. And besides, I haven't stepped in a pile of shit for quite a while." Reynolds laughed nervously, glanced out the front window at the dark, the splatters of rain and sleet. He could imagine that green Ford sedan pulling quietly to a stop outside.

"But let's not make this a social visit. Talk fast, brother. Let me know what I can do." Reynolds reached for the bottle, offered it to Perry, who shook his head.

"I'll come clean," Perry said, and he tried to dry his hands on the legs of his pants. Reynolds handed him a towel from the counter.

Perry started off in the middle somewhere, telling Reynolds how this wasn't the first time he had met Skinny and his pals at the boat ramp below, then he brought in the safe house, and the little militia group he had organized.

Then Perry told Reynolds about the half load of guns out back, and Reynolds muttered, "Oh shit," realizing at that moment that now the feds could seize his trailer and his store, and he would be in deep himself. Aiding and abetting and all that crap flew through his mind—and he regretted that quick flash of brotherly loyalty he had felt.

Perry quietly sighed, admitting his growing disillusionment with the whole thing, but how, by now, he was hooked into the extra money, especially with his contract to teach all at once probationary. "Everything suddenly started to slide, and pretty soon I lost my balance, I guess."

"Damn, Perry," Reynolds said, when his brother had finished, "when you do it you don't go half-ass." Then Reynolds told Perry about Kemp, the ATF man, how he had poked around there that Saturday. How that was almost surely him in the Ford sedan tonight. "What the hell can you do?"

"Well, I can't stay here," Perry said, and he started pacing around, moving with that peculiar bounce of a walk. "And I've got too much money tied up in this deal—I need to make a phone call, maybe I can go ahead and collect later tonight." He looked around, spotted the pay phone on the wall. Then he seemed to think it through, saw himself on the road with those guns. By now Kemp would have called in plenty of help to watch the roads, knowing, whether he caught up with Skinny or not, that there was another fish or two to land out by the lake.

By morning, if not before, they would be checking Perry at his house. From what Reynolds had told him Perry realized that somehow they were on to him. There was an informer out there—maybe the Dallas connection, maybe one of his own militia, somebody he had pissed off—and two or three possibilities flashed through his mind. But that didn't matter now.

"Yeah, Perry," Reynolds said, "You damned sure need to move the rest of those guns. Shit, man, just dump them."

"Hell, Reynolds, that's easy for you to say. It's not your money." Perry moved over to the window, checked the road, checked the blackness of the sky. All Reynolds could see from where he stood was Perry's desperate reflection.

Reynolds moved to the window, and Perry turned towards him. Reynolds put his hands on his brother's shoulders. "How much is that load of guns worth?" he asked.

"I paid two grand. They should bring three, if I can collect, if I can deliver the rest."

"That's not what I mean. How much are they really worth?"

Perry looked at his brother a moment. To Reynolds he seemed confused or impatient or angry. Maybe all three. "Okay. You're right," Perry said, looking past Reynolds. "But I need your help."

Reynolds nodded slowly. Then with a quick shrug he turned and jogged to the trailer for his boots and his hat. By then Perry had the truck started.

They circled around Reynolds' trailer house, and in the dark, Perry eased the truck and the boat back down the gravel road to the ramp. Perry backed the trailer into the lake until the boat almost floated, and Reynolds loosened the winch and pushed the boat free.

"Toss me your keys," Reynolds demanded, and Perry did, and in a minute Reynolds eased the truck, with the empty trailer rattling behind, up the hill. He pulled around the back of the trailer and found an overgrown two-rut road that led to an abandoned gravel pit. He gunned the truck, overrunning a scrabble of brush and weeds until the truck stalled up against a post-oak sprout. Reynolds figured the truck might need a new paint job, but that was Perry's problem.

Back down at the boat ramp Perry held the boat steady and Reynolds splashed a couple of steps and pulled himself in, tumbling over the rest of the shrink wrapped guns in the dark.

"Damn, almighty shit," Reynolds muttered, breathing hard. Then with a sputter the engine jerked to life and Perry turned the nose of the boat north.

He kept near the shoreline, following the dark outline of trees to his left. Reynolds was colder than shit, wished he'd had the presence of mind to slip a half pint of whiskey into his jacket pocket.

In less than an hour Perry found the inlet that led to the

safe house, and turned the nose of the boat to his left. He slowed the engine to a purr. "It's here," he said. "Up this creek a ways. There's a trail. The safe house is back in the woods a pretty good piece. In a clearing."

"They'll find it," Reynolds said. He shifted, rocking the boat a little. He could no longer feel his feet. "They know you have a boat. You gonna tell them you were running a trot line? Shit. They'll have a chopper out here, spot your place in no time at all."

Perry got quiet. Reynolds could tell he must be thinking of alternative plans. Perry might have a wacky view of the way the world works—hell, that was genetic, Reynolds figured—but he was no redneck dumbass.

Perry cut the motor, needed the quiet so he could think. Reynolds was right, when the feds get after you, having a safe house back in the woods wasn't going to cut it. They would find the cabin and the guns and Perry would be history.

There was only one way. Perry started the outboard motor up again, turned the boat away from the dark line of trees and putted slowly towards the center of the lake.

Reynolds sat there, now puzzled, but willing to go along on another crazy ride.

Perry kept looking back, lining up with a promontory of land he could barely make out behind him. Then he shut down the engine and for a moment they drifted.

In a minute Reynolds felt Perry lean forward and then there was a grunt and a big splash, and for an instant Reynolds thought Perry might have gone overboard. But then he saw Perry standing, a dark shadow above him, bending and grabbing and heaving the bundles of guns into the lake. In a few moments they were gone. "That was the channel, I hope," Perry said.

"Deep enough, I'll bet," Reynolds said.

"Okay, now let's take a hike," and Perry's voice had lightened. "I'll dump them all. A couple of trips and we can do it."

"Good boy," Reynolds said. This was just what he had in mind, the only possible way out for Perry, as he saw things. "I mean, good man," Reynolds caught himself, and Perry gave a little laugh. Reynolds hadn't thought of it before, but that was the first time he had heard Perry laugh for years.

The trail to the safe house was slow going in the dark, the way soft and slick, and the branches above them dumped icy water down Reynolds' back, but together they made it and in three trips toted out a couple of dozen rifles from the safe house to the boat, and went back for the crates of ammunition.

Perry used a flashlight he kept there to give the place a final check, and Reynolds picked up quick glimpses of some sleeping bags and several five-gallon plastic jugs of water, a couple of rows of canned beans and chili on a shelf.

In the center of the room sat a spindly card table, some file folders in a cardboard box on the plank floor. Lots of spider webs. The scurry of a rat across a rafter.

The sleet had started again, pecking lightly on the tin roof while Perry made his way inside the safe house. He found a can of kerosene, and sprinkled it on the plywood walls and around the floor. He stepped outside, still holding the empty can down at his side. He hesitated a moment, and Reynolds recognized that moment, one when everything you have dreamed—whether it is a marriage or a bank or a safe house—is about to go up in flames. Then Perry gestured with the light, and Reynolds stepped inside. "Careful," Perry said, and in a minute Reynolds had touched the flame of his lighter in a half dozen places, then backed out of the door, away from the quick-rush of crackle and flash.

They moved off for a minute, watching, waiting until the heat drove them back. "Let's get the hell out of here," Reynolds said, and together they made their way to the trail, their shadows flickering before them.

FOURTEEN

A FRIDAY evening in March. Reynolds glanced at the waterfall clock on the wall; it was just before 8:40 bar time. He checked the display he was putting together, some Texas wines from the hill country, a little pricey, he figured, but you had to be progressive, lead the way, or Lake City Liquors would be just another liquor store.

A few minutes earlier the green ATF sedan had cruised by. Kemp slowed his car, flashed a spotlight across the boat ramp below, and moved on across the bridge where he turned around at the gravel pull-off where he had flushed Snider out of his lookout a few weeks before.

On that dark night of the ice storm no one had spotted the fire back in the woods and by morning the rain had smothered the ashes. Reynolds figured that the trees and vines and briars would reclaim the rubble in another season. The next day Kemp had stopped by for a chat, but all of the action of the night before had occurred well after 9:00, after, Reynolds claimed with a straight face, he had locked the place down and had retreated to his trailer. "A man would have to be crazy," Reynolds told Kemp, "to go out in that kind of weather."

"Yeah," Kemp said, suspicion in his voice. "He would."

Reynolds had watched from the window while Kemp pulled his car away from the liquor store and eased it down the incline to the boat ramp. The lawman worked his way back and forth across the shoreline, squatting on his haunches here and there, finally pulling his sedan back up to the road and driving away. The rain had been a blessing, washing tire prints and footprints into mushy indentations, shadows of clay and mud.

One of these days, Reynolds knew, a fisherman would hook a couple of shrink wrapped AK-47s and things would stir back up, but time and the wash of water would hold their secret.

Perry wouldn't be clear for a while, and the whole thing could catch up with him. But if Kemp had stopped Skinny and Fat Hand and Shadow that night, Reynolds would have heard something by now. Those three were pros, and wouldn't risk another call to Perry, not to nickel-and-dime a few modified automatic weapons.

Perry had told Reynolds that he still didn't know who put the finger on him, but whoever it was obviously didn't know about the safe house, or Kemp and his cronies would have been there first thing. "Bar talk," Perry figured. "Some sloppy-mouthed bar talk tipped the feds." Something overheard, a little too much said over a game of eight ball some angry night.

Perry acknowledged he would have to watch his back for a while and kick the shit off of his boots before he stepped inside the classroom, but Reynolds figured his brother knew enough to stay ex-Marine straight if he had to.

For a few days Reynolds waited for Perry to say something more—a simple thanks, some gesture, some acknowledgement to his brother for helping him out in a tight. But there was nothing, and finally Reynolds shrugged it off. The tangled resentments of brothers run deep.

In a few minutes Reynolds would turn the sign in the window to "Nope," hit the lights and put on some music to mellow out by. UPS Carl had dropped off a couple of new tapes earlier today, so Reynolds could implement his latest strategy. He would play light stuff during the day, a little country—not Garth Brooks, who reminded him of Joy, and not Willie Nelson, who brought up Sheila's blue eyes that never, ever cried in the rain—but something harmless for the fisher boys who stopped by, headed out on the lake to get drunked up.

Reynolds would keep the other tape ready, just in case.

Just before nine a Jeep Waggoneer pulled up outside in the dark. The driver, some woman, Reynolds could tell, hurried up the steps and in a moment was inside with a bang of the door.

She stood there in the front of the store, her hands on her hips. The first time she had been in, Reynolds knew, from the way she glanced around, hunting for something.

Besides, Reynolds would have remembered her, for she had brassy good looks, and class, a no-nonsense sort of stance that spelled sureness and trouble at the same time.

"Do you have any California wines?" she asked. She glanced at her watch. "I didn't think I was going to make it."

A Dallas woman, North Dallas. Reynolds could tell, the slightly nasal niceness that her mama had taught her, an impatient boldness that she couldn't hide.

Reynolds pulled himself straight, pointed to the far aisle.

"I suggest the Stag's Leap," he said, "unless you want some-thing more complex, not as fruity."

The woman cocked her head sideways a moment, took Reynolds in, then moved quickly around the counter.

Almost without looking Reynolds eased his new tape in, and in a few seconds the Dave Brubeck Quartet started in on "Comes Once in a Lifetime." He turned it up a little and the music filled the room. Romantically sophisticated, Reynolds thought.

The woman across the room bent down, then straightened back up. She studied this wine label and then that one. In a bit she glanced quickly over at Reynolds and then back down. She had the look of a woman who had come of age in the seventies, with Shelia's shoulder length hair, turned up on the ends. Not frosted, though. Red. Bottle red, probably, but a classy job, natural against the paleness of her face.

She used glasses to read the labels, holding them in one hand, fumbling each time she put them back on. She was tall and trim, and Reynolds could imagine her heading out most mornings to jazzercise or tennis lessons or swimming at some Dallas country club.

"Nice selection," she said, holding up a bottle of red. "Nice music, too. What is that, anyway?"

"Brubeck," Reynolds said. "You want a red, you might try the Merlot."

"Oh," she said, disappearing behind the shelves once again. She came up with a bottle in one hand, her glasses in the other. "This?"

Reynolds nodded, and in a minute she came his way with three bottles, one in each hand, one tucked under her arm. She looked terrific, Reynolds thought, with her Mexican-yellow, scooped-neck blouse and jeans. She wore pointy-toed boots that had been stitched from the skin of some unfortunate reptile and dyed red.

"Well," she said, "this is such a nice surprise. I thought I'd have to run back up to Dallas in the morning. I'm throwing a little party tomorrow afternoon, and somehow got off without the wine. I mean I rolled out the pasta and was letting it dry, and reached for my wine glass, and then it hit me. Oh, my God, almost 9:00 and no wine. Not even for tonight—which I guess I could have survived—but then tomorrow I would have been stuck there, with the osso bucco needing to simmer for hours. Well, you have surely saved my life." She laughed and Reynolds tipped his imaginary hat in an exaggerated way.

"That's why I'm here, ma'am." Time to make your move, he thought, and extended his hand. "Reynolds," he said.

She hesitated a moment, flushed just a little, but kept her poise, and stayed in control. She shook his hand and quickly pulled it back. "Reynolds? Is there more?"

"Is that enough?" he asked.

"I'm Charity Browning," she said. "I just finished a lake house over on Five Oaks. What a nightmare. I'll never do that again," she said. "Not alone."

Reynolds nodded, picked up on that "alone" business. "It's nice over there," he said. "Actually, I financed that subdivision when the Bandy boys opened it up, eight, nine years ago."

She raised her thin eyebrows, brown mascara underneath a sprinkling of fine, reddish hairs. She wasn't going to let Reynolds' remark slide by. She was a woman attuned to finances, he could tell.

"Well, my bank financed them," he went on. "I headed up Farmers and Merchants, over in Cottonwood back then."

"I see," she said.

Reynolds rang up the wine, wiped each bottle down, sacked them separately, twisted the sack tops, and cradled them inside a sturdy brown paper bag with handles.

Charity swept one arm around the bag, but stood there for a moment, her arm resting on the counter. "I do like that music," she said. "It's such a surprise, you know. I mean. . . ." She looked around at the liquor store, the beer signs, the rack of Dallas Cowboy gimme caps, the shelf of catfish blood bait.

Reynolds nodded. He leaned forward a little, his voice conspiratorial. "I play the good stuff after nine. After I close. Afraid somebody will hear it and turn me in."

She laughed. "Well, if it's better than this, I'd like to hear it, and I certainly wouldn't turn you in. Maybe award you a medal." She looked at Reynolds straight on, unblinking. A dare. Reynolds never backed away from a dare. Although he should have more than once, he knew.

"I don't drink wine after nine," Reynolds said. "I'm an Old Fitz sort of a guy. But I can put a bottle in the cooler," he said. "Whatever you like. It is Friday night."

"Well, I don't think so," Charity said. "I have a bunch of girls coming down from Dallas tomorrow, mid-afternoon." She pulled the sack of wine to her chest. She wagged her head a little, as if she were thinking, "on the one hand this, and on the other hand that."

"Whatever," Reynolds said. "You can hang around, I'll be shutting the place down pretty soon. Or you could drop back by, if that works better. I'll be here, be playing my music, anyway. If you can come back over, the blinds will be drawn, but I'll be here, sipping along. I got a new tape today. Thought I'd give it the old Reynolds' critique tonight. Maybe you could help."

"Well, I appreciate the invitation, but I'd better not, I guess. And besides, I don't really even know who you are."

"One bad character," Reynolds said with a laugh.

She laughed, too. "Not too bad, I'll bet."

"I'll be here until midnight," Reynolds said, with a wave of his hand. "Regardless."

In a moment she was gone, striding hard across the wooden floor in her boots, then outside, the screen door banging behind her. She wheeled the Wagoneer backwards, gave a vague little wave towards the store, and with a spin of her tires was onto the asphalt road. Reynolds watched the tail-lights of her Jeep as it hurried across the bridge. In a couple of minutes it had topped the far hill and disappeared.

Reynolds put a couple of bottles of wine—a Chardonnay and a pricey-as-shit Pinot Grigio, from Italy—in the cooler. He locked up and swept the floor, making bold sweeps with the broom. Then he hurried back to the trailer. He brushed his teeth, and started to change his shirt, but decided against it. Reynolds knew not to appear too eager. She probably wouldn't show up again, anyway.

Back in the store he lowered the front blinds, made sure the "Nope" sign was in place, and then he went through his tapes. He would pretend that the Kronos tangos he liked so much were new, he decided, and took that tape out, left it beside the boom box under the counter.

Reynolds retrieved his bottle of Old Fitz 1849 and poured a short drink. He reached for his cigarettes, but thought bet-ter of it. May be time for a reform or two. He sipped the Old Fitz. One reform at a time, he figured.

Reynolds kicked off his shoes and in his sock feet slid over to the window that opened across the lake. He thought of his

daddy, up the lake those six dark miles, and hoped his perpetual motion machine was running, clicking and swishing
away. Reynolds wanted it to run forever. His daddy, too.

He gazed down at the boat landing, then over the blackness of the lake to where the road disappeared. Tonight it felt
sufficient to be here. The liquor store had grown on him;
these after-hours times with good music and a drink were
special. A decent place to sleep out back. A man needs a place
like this, he thought. This may, in fact, be all that a man needs.

Reynolds sipped on his whiskey and rocked gently as
another cut on the Brubeck tape began. He checked his
reflection in the window, all of a sudden seeing himself dif-
ferently than before, now in the dim glow of the beer sign
lights. Maybe he was different. "Reynolds," he said out loud,
"you are a changed man."

Maybe he would get Stick to mind the store for a couple
of days and drive out to Odessa, spend some time with his
boys. And when he got back, maybe he would drop by to see
Perry, spend some time with him—without expectations.
And he would contact Joy, maybe over a burger at the Next
to Nowhere Cafe, and tell her to forget the fifty dollars she
owed him. Why not? And women? Maybe he would take
some time off from women, too.

He could call Sheila, tell her about this new Reynolds, see
what she thought. "Shit," he said with a shake of his head.
Then he laughed out loud.

Reynolds stood at the window for a long time, swaying
easily to the rhythms of the soft jazz. He no longer cared if
Charity Browning came back around. Not tonight, anyway.
He stared out over the water, content with himself, with the
possibilities of Reynolds and his new world.

Then something caught his eye, and he turned towards the dark ribbon of road, suddenly alert to a pair of headlights that topped the far away hill, hurrying his way.